CASE FILES OF THE WILKINSON NATIONAL DETECTIVE AGENCY

Also by Alexandria Blaelock

SHORT STORY COLLECTIONS
The Haunting of Hayward Hall
Lovelorn, Lovestruck and Love at First Sight
Common or Garden Variety Heroes

FICTION
That Love Nonsense

MS BLAELOCK'S BOOKS
Stress Free Dinner Parties
Signature Wardrobe Planning
Holistic Personal Finance
Minimally Viable Housekeeping
Planning a Life Worth Living

A SELECTION OF AVAILABLE
SHORT STORIES
Alma's Grace
Balancing the Book
Bygone Boyfriend
Fate in Your Hands
Kiss of Death
Lady of the Looking Glass
Life in the Security Directorate
Love in the Security Directorate
Morning Star, Evening Star, Superstar
Needy Bitch
Payton's Run
Secret Singer
Shining Star
Ship in a Bottle
Simone Says Hands in the Air
The Day the Schedule Broke

CASE FILES OF THE WILKINSON NATIONAL DETECTIVE AGENCY

ALEXANDRIA BLAELOCK

BlueMere Books
MELBOURNE, AUSTRALIA

For permission requests, please contact enquiries@bluemerebooks.com.

Ordering Information:
Discounts are available on quantity purchases. For details, contact orders@bluemerebooks.com.

Case Files of the Wilkinson National Detective Agency/
Alexandria Blaelock
hardback ISBN: 978-1-925749-73-1
paperback ISBN: 978-1-925749-74-8
digital ISBN: 978-1-925749-75-5

Book Layout © BookDesignTemplates.com

Contents

INTRODUCTION

When I was young, I used to watch a lot of Westerns with my Dad, who was a huge John Wayne fan.

Imagine if you can, a small, drunk man with a broad Glaswegian accent shouting "Howdy pardner," adjusting his imaginary Stetson as he performed his best party trick.

I expect he sounded exactly like John Wayne in his head.

And through him, I was introduced to the Pinkerton National Detective Agency, whose agents were commonly known as Pinkertons.

I've been fascinated by the Pinkertons since I was small. Which is kind of funny because they're American and we're not.

But there's something exciting about a detective agency that's kind of like I imagine a detective agency headed by Sherlock Holmes would be like.

An agency solving crimes with deductive reasoning, *and* guns.

Maybe, just maybe, Conan Doyle (1859 – 1930) was a little inspired by Alan Pinkerton (1819 – 1884).

Pinkerton set up his agency in 1850, and originally specialised in train robberies, but was mainly known for thwarting an assassination attempt on President-elect Abraham Lincoln.

Not that Pinkertons were crime solving masterminds like Sherlock Holmes, or even, for the want of a better term, uniformly "good" men and women.

And not that the organisation didn't do some things I think were kind of awful. Like infiltrating and intimidating unions, and strike breaking for those who could afford to pay them.

The Pinkertons existed at a particular time, and wouldn't have the same kind of mystique at any other time than right there in the wildest times of the wild wild west.

And I suppose, if you wanted justice, you were kind of stuck with them as there wasn't much in the way of Police forces as we know them now.

Australia, being a penal colony, was policed by English marines; there to keep the convicts down.

Though in our early days, the country's currency supply was so short, the marines were paid in goods, the most popular being rum. And while the 1808 Rum Rebellion was more of an uprising by the civil and military elites against the Governor, than about the rum...

As a country populated mainly by unionists, Fenians and petty thieves, we were the kind of people who lionised the underdogs; taking bushrangers to be political rebels or freedom fighters.

With established police forces, there wasn't much of a demand for private investigators until around the 1880s.

Generally, they focused on divorce cases, where corroborated evidence of adultery was pretty much the only way you were going to get a divorce.

Though without any regulation or licensing, it's not hard to imagine the social scene was ripe for a bit of blackmail, perjury and criminal trespass.

It wasn't until 1951 that private investigators were required to register and obtain a license to work.

Nowadays, they specialise in investigations of fact, surveillance and missing persons, mainly for insurances, financial losses, and contractual disputes. Most of them work in larger firms.

But I still wonder what an Australian version of the Pinkertons might be like now.

So, I invented the Wilkinson National Detective Agency, established in 1889.

I think working in an established corporate environment would be quite different to working for yourself...

So, for this mystery collection, I've tried to imagine working within corporate guidelines and policies. And how they might protect and hinder you.

First, Dot Sayers on her first job, doing background checks discovers something's not quite right about the target.

Then former cop Phoebe Swan, hired by the parents of a dead girl to solve the case that got away.

Followed by Shirley Weaving who's not cut out for normal investigations, but when something's not quite right, she's your girl.

And Susan Murray's following a crime kingpin until he starts following her!

Finally, Lily White investigates her grandfather's mysterious gangland murder.

So, here are five brand new private eye mysteries. I hope you enjoy them.

Alexandria Blaelock
Melbourne, Australia
July 2021

P.S., in case you wondered, the Pinkertons still exist today, as a subsidiary of Swedish based security services group Securitas AB.

Dot Sayers sat at her desk, huffed on the plastic card that was her new class A Private Security licence, and buffed it with her sleeve. She was now a fully licensed private investigator!

Not criminal investigations, her Investigative Services course had insisted, only civil investigations. Like insurance fraud, missing persons, or general security and background checks.

She sat up, looking over her tiny cubicle's grey soundproof walls like a meerkat, for someone to share her excitement with. But all she saw was the tops of heads, bent deep over their work.

The Collins Street office of the Wilkinson National Detective Agency (est. 1889), was crowded with seemingly hundreds of other tiny grey cubicles resting on a floor of grey carpet.

If you weren't ready for it when you walked in, the whole floor blended into a kind of uniform greyness, and with no differentiation of features;

nothing to distinguish any one cubicle from the mass of greyness.

Like walking into the middle of a cool, dark storm cloud, without the wetness.

Though storm clouds didn't usually smell like someone's leftover curry.

The sound of busy workers conducting phone interviews was a low-level hum around her, reminding her of the sleepy drone of a beehive on a warm summer day.

And in a way, that's what they were.

Hundreds of tiny drones, undertaking desk checks and verifications on an industrial scale. Like cold callers, except with relevant qualifications and some self-respect.

Nonetheless, Dot smiled and slotted the card in the top row of her computer keyboard, leaning against the function keys and patting it lightly into place. She was excited to have finally made it.

She pulled the stack of background checks towards her, tried to set the phone headset more comfortably on her head, and prepared to make her first call.

It might be grunt work for others, but for her, it was the first step on the long, glorious ladder to the big time.

Dot was named after grandmother Spencer, or Dotty as she was known, who was named after Dorothy L. Sayers.

For most of her childhood, she'd resented the old-fashioned name. When the jokes and taunts found her in school, she'd been prepared to be proud of her connection with the "original" Dorothy Sayers, but when she'd quizzed her parents, they'd confessed their ignorance.

Which somehow made it even worse.

She'd intended to change it as soon as she was old enough. But Dotty doted on her, and after she'd died, Dot came round to the name. Hoping to live up to both Dotty's and the "original's" example.

In fact, she adopted the circle as her signature icon and had hundreds of necklaces, earrings and hair accessories to dress up her otherwise plain, block, deep coloured clothing.

She dialled the first number, explained she was doing a background check for an employer, that she had the candidate's permission. Receiving their permission, she started working her way through the questionnaire, noting the answers on the form in permanent ink.

At the end of the day, she gathered up her files and reported in to her boss/mentor/supervising investigator Steve.

"Come," he said when she knocked on his door.

He was an older man, somewhere between middle-aged and ancient. His fierce green gaze was amplified by his horn-rimmed spectacles, and his eyebrow clenching frown made him look a bit like what she imagined an old-fashioned boy's school headmaster might look like.

His office was almost exactly like her cubicle, but with a larger chair, a window view and a longer desk.

And no neighbours.

She shut the door behind her and sat on the edge of one of the chairs facing him.

"So, how was your first day?" he asked.

"Fine..." She coughed a little to find her voice, "fine thank you, no problems."

"Good. And how did you get on?" he asked.

"Well," she said, putting the completed files on his desk. "I've done about a hundred files now," she said, knowing perfectly well she hadn't done anywhere near half that amount, "and they're all fine and straightforward except this one." She tapped the file on top of the pile labelled John Anderson.

"What makes you say that?" he asked, leaning forward to pick it up, and flip through it."

"I don't know," she shrugged, "the answers from each of the businesses were almost the same. It all seemed a bit down pat, a bit too positive. Like they'd memorised their parts and were reciting them back to me."

"Well, it all looks fine to me."

Dot slumped a very little as he leaned forward to look at her.

Then she tried again, "his last job was a few months ago, so it's possible they've forgotten what he was like. Or that he's really bad at his job, and his referees were glad to get rid of him. Or that... Oh, I don't know.

Steve relaxed back into his chair, looking at her, tapping the file against his lip as he considered what to do.

"Look, I don't see an issue," he said, "but you're the one who makes the call about whether to investigate further. I think it's a waste of time, but I'm going to give this back to you to do some more digging. Then you'll learn when to trust your gut and when not to."

He offered her the file and she stood up to receive it.

"Thanks Steve, I won't let you down."

He held the one file a moment longer, "it's not a priority, so don't fall behind in your regular work," he said before he let it go.

Dot was so excited to take it back she almost curtsied.

She took the files back to the record store, noting the return of the Anderson file to her the next day. Then she cleared her desk, making sure to strictly adhere to the policy, by locking all her pens and papers in the drawer.

She glanced around, and seeing no one, did a little fist punch in the air. She'd survived her first day on the job, had a file of her own to investigate further, and was on her way to becoming a top-notch private investigator.

The next day she was so excited to get to work and make a start, she woke before her alarm went off, left her apartment well before she needed to, and got off the tram a few stops early because it was taking too long.

She strode happily down the footpath; almost skipping, but too purposefully to be considered so frivolously.

And because she didn't anticipate a break until lunchtime, she picked up a latte and a small hedgehog slice, assuring the barista *everything* was fine and she hoped he was too.

All that and still in the office a little before she was due, though she had to wait a little while at the records office to receive the day's files. And then took a little more time to find her desk again.

She set aside the files, took a sip of her coffee and looked at the Anderson file again. She couldn't pin her nebulous feeling of suspicion down to any one thing. It was more the overall vibe.

The fingerprints were not in the file, so she couldn't check those, but she could request a Federal Police and credit check.

Both would require a payment she wasn't authorised to make, and take around a week, but they were something further to consider.

The candidate had listed three previous employers, they looked to be small or maybe small-to-medium businesses, though her reference checks had not included anyone from a senior position, so she grabbed a pad of file notes and a pen, and looked them up on the internet.

At first glance, the first website seemed legitimate, with the Australian Business Number, addresses, phone numbers, and details of the partners. But when she looked through some of the pages, they didn't make any sense in the context of the front page. A bit like random grab bags of information that would do for a quick glance.

She jotted down the details and her thoughts, then moved on to the next site.

The second website included the same basic information but was just a landing page inviting you to fill in the contact form. There was so little information it seemed more legitimate than the first, but still, she couldn't quiet that nagging voice in her head.

When she looked at the site again, she realised the phone number was different by one digit from that listed on the reference she'd called the previous day.

Before she could give herself too long to think about it, she put her headset on and dialled the number.

It rang several times.

She was slightly surprised an answering machine hadn't kicked in - a legitimate business that wanted to make money would have answered or queued an automatic system by now.

Dot was about to hang up when someone answered the phone.

"Hello?" an old, thin voice answered.

"Oh, hello! My name's Dot Sayers, I called yesterday to do a reference check?"

There was a long silence at the other end of the phone.

"Hello? I'm calling about John Anderson?"

The silence continued?

"Are you there?"

"No.

"No.

"No. There's no one here by that name."

"I'm so sorry to bother you then. Goodbye."

And she hung up.

And took a deep breath.

It was entirely possible for the website to contain an error.

But.

She wrote the information on her notes along with the result of the second call

The third website had ABN, but no addresses or phone numbers, only a contact form. When she accidentally clicked on the background image, she was directed to a template page still containing the Lorum ipsem text.

It was possible the businesses were not up-to-date with the current online sales and marketing practises, but that all three sites did not at least look professional seemed suspicious.

And one admin manager position was pretty much like the next, aside from the levels of confidential information you might expect to have access to at the client's company.

She did a quick, free Securities Commission search for each business and noted the owner names they were listed under weren't suspicious, aside from being Smiths, Jones, and Lee, which were some of the most common names in Australia.

Dot drummed her fingers on her desk, wondering what to do next, not willing to give up so soon.

And then she smiled and looked up the business addresses and checked the street view.

Admittedly the view was probably out of date, but she noted none of the business on street view were the same as the business names she was investigating. The first one was a house, the second a warehouse, and the third a small accountancy firm.

None of them looked to be on the scale of size that would require a manager for several admin staff, though one admin person might be called the admin manager for the sake of making a tiny business seem a bigger concern.

Getting more detailed business information seemed the next step, but again required a payment she was not authorised to make.

Then again, was that that going too far when she was assessing John Anderson for a position with her client?

Though, it could mean Anderson had fabricated the references for the purpose of fraudulently gaining a position at the company.

Potentially, Anderson had backers who'd set up, or at least bought shelf companies.

Not that a company with no previous history was suspicious, but overall, she was coming up with too many red flags.

By this point, Dot was convinced John Anderson, if that was his real name, had something to hide. But it had taken her just short of an hour to get this far, and she still had a day's worth of background checks to do.

She didn't think Steve would be happy about that.

Dot updated the file note with her findings, and her recommendation to proceed with personal criminal and credit checks for the candidate, and registration histories for the businesses.

She popped the files in her drawer, locked it, and went for a brisk walk around the floor. On the second lap, she stopped at the bathroom and the kitchen for instant coffee, then went back to her desk to do the reference checks.

The rest of the day passed without anything suspicious presenting itself, and it was time to check in with Steve, almost before she knew it. She almost danced to the door and tapped on the door with a smart rhythm.

"How are you getting along Dot? No problems or queries?"

"No, it's going well. I'm on target with the background checks."

"And what about the Anderson file?"

She grinned, "I think what I've discovered pretty much rules John Anderson out of proceeding to the next level of interviews."

"Okay, what are your grounds?"

"I've done some cursory checks of the websites of the businesses that employed him, and the information on-site doesn't tally up with the street view. One of the numbers on the second site is different to that on the reference and connects to something that sounds like a confused old man.

"If one of the websites was faulty that would be one thing, but all of them? It's just too coincidental."

"Go on."

"Our client is dealing with classified secrets, and the potential of a fraudulent application is too great a risk for the company to permit this early in the process."

"And if this applicant was a preferred candidate who was invited to apply?"

Dot thought considered the options.

"Then it would be necessary to look a little deeper to uncover evidence of fraud."

"And how would you do that?"

She listed them off on her fingers, "One, have an internal investigator verify the 100 points check in person to validate that the documents do exist and at least appear genuine. Then order copies from the original sources to validate them from central records.

"Two, order Federal Police and credit reference file checks.

"Three, order detailed business checks to verify the company details."

"Good work," Steve said with a small congratulatory smile, "I'll hold onto this and order the checks you recommend. Then I'll transfer the file to investigations, and mark it for return to you.

"Our investigators usually sight the original identification documents when they take the fingerprints anyway, and the file is updated with their in-person impressions at the time.

"Anderson will probably fall over himself to get this done, and it will seem to him that everything is proceeding well.

"And a good call with this one. Imagine if you had let it go when I first challenged you on this."

Dot smiled and bowed her head a little at the praise.

"If there's nothing else?"

She shook her head, and he indicated the files. She picked them up and walked to the door.

"Wait." She shifted the files to rest on her hip and frowned as she thought through the implications of a "preferred" candidate.

"If Anderson was recommended by someone inside the company, we should look into that person as well."

Steve tilted his head quizzically.

"Well, perhaps Anderson has some kind of leverage over that person. Like a gambling debt, or drug habit, or compromising photographs."

Steve narrowed his eyes at her, and then pointed at the chair, "elaborate."

"If you needed access to the company to retrieve some kind of information, one of the easiest ways would be to blackmail them."

"Wouldn't you just approach a senior officer and get to know them?"

"Well, that's one way, but look at us here at Wilkinson's. Our fields of interest and responsibility are quite narrow, taking out a Senior Executive wouldn't do any good if it wasn't the right one…

"Wait a minute, how did the vacancy come about?"

Steve typed something on his computer, paused, and said, "ski accident."

They looked at each other for a moment as the stakes raised around them.

"Well, that puts a slightly different complexion on things doesn't it?" he asked.

Dot scrubbed her face with both hands, "it's like some kind of spy movie. I feel like John Anderson isn't going to be this guy's real name, don't you?"

"I'm sorry. At this point, I'm going to have to take this file from you and hand it on to someone more appropriate than a new employee on her second day at work."

"But—"

Steve stood up, "in the usual scheme of things you would have performed the reference checks and that's all. You don't have the knowledge or experience to carry this out any further."

Dot stood, "but—"

"I'm sorry. I'll keep you informed."

She had no option but to nod and leave the office. Her feet dragging, she deposited the files back to the records office, cleared her desk and left the building with a heavy heart.

With a night to stew it over, the next day she went into work, resolute in her intention to see what else she could dig up.

Another latte, and another hedgehog from the café, another impatient dance in the queue for her files for the day.

And then she was ready for what she hoped would be a covert search for John Anderson.

Nothing overly suspicious in the search engines, though without access to a photo she couldn't really tell. The social media accounts seemed relatively recent, with few posts, but again that wasn't unusual. Some people took to them, and others didn't.

Inspired by Nancy Drew and Trixie Belden, her intention to become a private investigator had ruled out many things people her age adopted. Like social media, and who's to say John Anderson wasn't the same.

And then the internet cut out.

In fact, it wasn't just the internet, it was her whole computer.

As if someone had just thrown a switch and shut it down.

She lifted her head to look up and around the office, and no one else seemed to be alert or alarmed by a shutdown.

And as she looked around, she noticed the cameras for the first time.

The closest one had a little red light that was blinking at her.

So, her activities had not been as covert as she's thought.

She nodded at the camera, put her headset on, and started making the day's calls.

That afternoon, when she met Steve for her usual daily review, she was filled with dread.

She curled inwards over the files clutched to her chest as she entered his office, expecting him to sack her.

"No problems?" he asked.

She swallowed and shook her head mutely.

"I know you've been looking up John Anderson. I understand you think you're some kind of Nancy Drew, but you must learn when you can go it alone, and when you need to call on specialist advice."

Feeling suddenly 12 years old again, she nodded mutely and refused to meet his eyes while she tried to remember what she'd written on her job application.

"For god's sake, even Nancy Drew got help now and again from Bess, George, and Ned!"

Surprised, she looked up at him.

"Daughters," he said and rolled his eyes.

Dot laughed.

"Okay, okay, I get it."

"We're good now?"

She nodded, and stood, collecting the files up.

"Dot?" he waited until she met his eyes, "you know you can ask me anything?"

He held her gaze for a long time, long enough to make the point.

So.

She could ask him anything, as long as it was the right question.

She nodded and turned away.

What was the right question for a girl on the third day of her new job?

With a night to think it over, she thought she might have the right question. Though it was probably quite impertinent for her fourth day at work.

She made her calls, and when the time came to report to Steve, her heart was pounding in her chest, and her mouth was dry.

Once the daily checks were out of the way, she asked her question, "Might I be permitted to attend the briefing meetings about the Anderson file?"

Steve looked at her steadily, reading her.

"A new investigations team has been formed to deal with Anderson, and I'm prepared to let you join it as admin support—"

She let out a noise that was half squeal and half sigh as she relaxed into the chair.

He smiled tolerantly, "but you must remember you don't own this investigation. You're just there to provide admin support."

"Thank you," she said, "I won't let you down."

"You'll still be on probation, so if you mess up, you'll be out the door."

He stood up and walked around the desk.

Dot stood up as he held out his hand, putting hers into his.

"This is probably goodbye. You'll be ready for a new challenge when the team finishes its investigation, and if you do well, the Investigations Division will put you where they need you."

"Thank you. I'm a little scared now that I'm..."

"Nonsense. You've got a good brain in your head, and if you keep doing what you do, you'll go far."

She wiped a tear from the corner of her eye. "Right. Well, I'll just drop this lot off and go."

"Yes. Clear your desk tonight, and start on Level 15 tomorrow."

Dot told herself not to get too excited. She was just starting to get comfortable in her job, and now she had another, with no idea what to expect.

But if there really was a career ladder, it seemed like she might have climbed the first rung already.

THE END

BLOOD AND BLOODY PROFANITY

P hoebe Swan stood, concealed by a grove of trees, looking down over the grave. The exhumation represented the worse possible outcome, of her worst possible case.

The morning sun shone brightly, the air quiet and still, without the hit of a breeze.

Just as it had been the day of almost sixteen-year-old Lette Walker's funeral.

Only without the scene of pink-clad mourners bellowing like cows at milking time.

Sweat trickled down her sides, making a mockery of her deodorant manufacturer's claim of 72 hours of dryness.

She *could* have worn something cooler and lighter than her black crepe pants suit, but black was how she felt as well as how she was.

Any other colour would have felt like a mockery.

She could see silhouettes against the brightly lit sides of the tent they worked within. Police clustered on one side, watching the gravediggers work.

Where they'd once lowered Lette out in the open, now they lifted her in private.

If only time reversed itself at the same moment.

She'd been the one who was supposed to find the kidnappers, catch them, and bloody well bang them up.

Before they killed the girl, and before they fled with the money.

And even though Inspector Mason had revealed the information to the kidnappers, she'd taken responsibility. She'd quit, while he'd stayed in the force, "earning" a promotion.

For the sake of future victims, she hoped he was incompetent and not corrupt. But regardless of how or why he did what he did, neither was a good outcome.

She'd chosen to suffer, and suffer she had throughout the intervening decade.

Moped for a while, then got her Private Security licence and joined the Wilkinson National Detective Agency. Established 1889.

Joining a long, and proud history that had come a long way since those early days of divorces, perjury, and trespass.

Because despite everything, she was still a good investigator. And still felt compelled to right the wrongs.

It was her habit to talk to Lette when she ran into an issue she needed to work through.

Because no one listens better than the dead.

And often a quiet moment with Lette did help clear the brain and get the neurons firing.

But if Lette wasn't there...

She watched the exhumation a little longer, wondering why, and who, and how it had come about.

And then she sighed and turned away, almost running straight into Lette's mother; Grace Walker, the last person she wanted to see.

Who'd lost half her body weight, and seemingly three-quarters of her wits in the decade since Phoebe had last seen her; when Lette had been laid to rest.

Phoebe nodded and attempted to walk past her, but Mrs Walker, wild grey hair standing on end, caught her sleeve in a surprisingly strong grip, effectively preventing her escape.

Phoebe turned her head to look at Mrs Walker, who said, "you can see we're bringing her out."

Not trusting her voice, she nodded.

"We want to know what happened."

Phoebe nodded again and attempted to walk away, but the older woman held her jacket fast.

"We don't want no uppity bloke telling us what's what this time. We want *you*.

Surely that had to be an exaggeration, she shook her head.

Mrs Walker shook the arm of Phoebe's jacket, and her arm with it.

"You. You always told us straight. You were always fair and reasonable until that Inspector turned up."

Phoebe cleared her throat, "I'm not with the Police anymore. I'm a Wilkinson investigator now."

"That's right. Private now."

"You can't just come to me; you'll have to go through the office. And I'm on another case anyway."

"We want you."

Phoebe sighed; she just wasn't getting through to the woman.

"Come with me, we'll sort something out."

《《 • 》》

Phoebe sat in a white interrogation room; no windows, no clocks, and grey linoleum on the floor. There was nothing, aside from the scuff marks on the walls to look at.

The room was furnished with a battered table, two chairs on one side, and a hard chair with one slightly bent leg on the other.

She was fairly sure it was an attempt to undermine her confidence.

The wonky chair was an old interrogation technique; most people couldn't sit still, or get comfortable, but would rock backwards and forwards as they tried to maintain their balance.

She, however, had learned a lot about bullying and intimidation during her time with Wilkinson's. She sat up; spine straight, feet firmly on the floor, leaning slightly back. She closed her eyes, folded her hands in her lap and waited.

Perfectly still.

Fortunately, she had plenty to think about.

Starting with how quickly Grace Walker had convinced her boss Sharon to allocate the case to her.

And what she'd said that had convinced Sharon to take all Phoebe's other cases away so she'd have no choice but to devote all her time and energy to Lette's case.

Not to mention, that Sharon had given her full access to all the resources and services Wilkinson's offered.

And biggest of all, what exactly Grace Walker hoped to achieve.

So, giving it the most charitable interpretation of events.

1. Lette had been kidnapped.

2. The kidnappers had demanded a ransom of $100,000.

3. The Walkers had taken out a loan.

4. Mason made the drop and walked away - in full view of at least six undercover Police Officers.

5. No one saw the moment when the money was taken.

6. The money was never recovered.

7. The kidnappers claimed not to have received the payoff.

8. A few days later, after a series of increasingly angry phone conversations, Lette's badly beaten body had been dumped.

9. The body was rushed through forensics, then released, and out the door to the funeral home.

10. Buried, in retrospect, with what seemed like indecent haste.

It was a harsh lesson for the Walkers - who had to deal with bankruptcy while they grieved.

But as far as anyone else was concerned, at least the body had been recovered, and they weren't left wondering.

So, at this point, she had to go back to basics.

And given the Walkers were funding the exhumation and subsequent forensic pathology...

She started listing the factors.

1. Was the body was in fact, Lette?

2. If not, who was it?

3. Why was she substituted for Lette?

4. How had the substitute died?

5. Where the hell was Lette?

Someone high up in Wilkinson's had leaned on someone high up in the Police, who had given her permission to view the file and her case notes to refresh her memory.

The door jerked open, and judging by the heavy tread, a large, male Police Officer strode in.

"Napping on the job eh Swan?" Mason asked.

She waited for a moment before opening her eyes, and looked up at him. Framing himself in the door.

Time had not been kind to his face, even if it had his shoulder. He'd let himself go; too many political dinners and not enough time in the gym.

She raised an eyebrow, "are you slumming it down here Superintendent Mason? Don't you have any big cases upstairs that need your attention more?"

He crossed the floor in two steps, and leaned one hip against the table, slapping the file against the other, "as the officer in charge of this investigation, I thought it prudent to at least see what you have."

"Wilkinson's has just allocated the case to me," she said, showing him her license card, but didn't let him remove it from her fingers, "I don't have anything to share yet."

He grunted, "well, I hope you don't mind, but I'll be watching you to ensure you don't remove anything from the file."

Phoebe smiled, a straight, thin smile - she'd been expecting that, "I'm not sure why you refused to prepare an evidence brief for the Walker's lawyers. That seems fishy to me."

He stood, and flung the file on the desk, "you have one hour."

Still smiling, she nodded, and pulled the wonky chair closer to the table.

He paced the length of one side of the room as she took out her daybook and opened the file at the beginning.

He paced along the second wall as she started to read, and jotted down her first note.

He paced out the third wall as she took her first photo of an evidence report.

He paced out the fourth wall, and she watched him from under the cover of her lowered eyelids.

So this was how he wanted to play it.

She was a little surer now that he had something to do with the disappearance of the money. Though she still had no proof.

She ignored him as he continued pacing in circles, clockwise then anticlockwise, occasionally knocking her chair, as she continued to study the file for the rest of the hour.

An alarm went off somewhere on his person, his watch or his phone, and he swooped on the file, knocking her phone to the floor.

She left it where it was, "I'll take my notebook and fountain pen if you please."

He made a show of reading over her notes, not that it mattered as she'd written it in her version of shorthand - almost indecipherable to herself let alone others.

She caught her fountain pen as he dropped it, hoping he hadn't bent the nib. There was next to nowhere left in Melbourne where she could fix it.

She swapped the lid from the post to the nib, collected her phone from the floor, and held out her hand for the book.

He dropped it on the desk and left the room.

Mason was as arrogant as ever.

But the tricks that had worked on her a decade ago, were useless now. She wasn't a probationary detective anymore. And he was nowhere near as impressive physically or intellectually.

She added a question to her list:

6. What the hell did Mason have to hide?

With the resources of Wilkinson's at her back, the next step was to visit the Victorian Institute of Forensic Medicine to see what they'd found.

She was escorted to a neat, clean meeting room by a young, and seemingly efficient man, "Dr Daniels is just finishing up her report and will be with you shortly. Can I get you something to drink?"

Phoebe declined, but he brought a jug of cold water and a couple of glasses on a tray anyway. It made her want coffee, but she didn't tell him she'd changed her mind.

He clearly had more important things to do.

At least this room had chairs with four even legs and an outside view over the Coroner's Court.

It could be considered comfortable, though its purpose wasn't to make hardened criminals confess.

She took out her daybook and started going through her notes.

"Hello," a tall, blonde woman said as she walked through the door and closed it behind her. "I'm Dr Jane Daniels, how are you?"

"Phoebe Swan, Wilkinson's Investigator," she said standing up to shake the woman's hand.

Jane laid a manilla folder on the table in front of Phoebe, "I don't believe this body is that of Lette Walker."

Phoebe frowned at the file without opening it, "what makes you say that?"

Jane sat at the table and poured two glasses of water, "This girl was riddled with cancer, and was receiving treatment for several months before she died, whereas Lette was fit and well.

"My guess is this body was taken from a funeral home sometime between the funeral and the inhumation."

Phoebe scratched her forehead with the tip of her capped fountain pen, "if she's not Lette do you know who she is?"

"Not yet, the body's been turned over to the Human Identification team."

"Is that not the kind of thing that should have been discovered in the first autopsy?"

"I would have thought so."

Phoebe listed out the sequence on her fingers, "so, someone, possibly the kidnappers, took a corpse from the mortuary.

"Smashed the girl's face in, hoping her identity wouldn't be discovered.

"Dressed her in Lette's clothes.

"The Pathologist rushed the autopsy.

"And the Police closed the investigation without actually investigating it."

Jane folded her hands on the desk, "I really wouldn't like to comment."

"I assume you're referring the body back to the Police?"

"We'll definitely have to at some point - we now have a missing person *and* an unidentified body.

"But as Wilkinson's commissioned the exhumation on behalf of the Walkers, we'll have to conclude your work first."

"I see, so for the moment, your team and I are the only ones who know about this?"

Jane nodded.

"Then you'll keep me up to date with the identity of the girl?"

"Of course. We've got some viable DNA, and we're running it through the databases we have access to, but the death was a decade ago, so I don't expect much from that avenue. I'll get someone to comb the registry of deaths to see if we can find a match."

"Thanks, that will definitely help. Anything else?"

"I've asked the team to do a facial reconstruction," Jane smiled, "If nothing else, given the girls are about the same age, it's possible the Walker's might know, and recognise her."

"I didn't see any reference to Lette's DNA analysis in the case file of the original investigation, but

I know took samples from Lette's hairbrush at the time."

"I'll see if there's any record of it here, but it might be quicker and easier to bring me something else. Even if it's just swabs from the parents."

"Sure, one way or another, I'll get something to you. Thank you for your time Jane."

"Glad to help. I had a sister around Lette Walker's age when the news broke. I looked at her, and I thought about Lette, and that's when I decided to become a doctor."

"I'm sure her mother would love to know that; something good came from Lette's death. Or I suppose we should now be saying Lette's disappearance."

"Then tell her. Only maybe not the bit where I was too nervous about meeting patients in person and transferred across to dead people."

Phoebe grinned, "yes. Dead people don't try to second guess you, or argue back."

Jane smiled in acknowledgement, "would you let me know how you're getting on with this case? If it's not too much trouble I mean."

"Of course. I'll be coming back to you with the DNA soon, should we make an appointment to catch each other up?"

"Good idea," she said, grinning as she pulled out her phone, "my diary gets crazy busy if I don't get things in it first."

Jane suggested a time, and Lette wrote it down. "I have to get back to work now," she said, "but the meeting room is booked for another half an hour if you want to stay here to look through the file."

"Thanks, I will."

"Until Wednesday then," Jane said.

Phoebe stood to shake her hand once more, "I'm looking forward to it."

With Jane out of the room, she sat and read through the file.

As it turned out, Lette had disappeared, and someone else had been buried in her place.

So, what exactly had happened to Lette?

It seemed the next step ought to be checking in with the Walkers to find out what *really* happened the day Lette went missing.

The Walkers' house was a small, tired, dusty weatherboard on a quarter acre of dry grass.

Crowded out by new, or half-constructed modern triplexes and building sites.

Not a tree, or a bush, or a bird to be seen.

The sun's heat reflected off the road, brick and asbestos fences, and the concrete façades of the neighbouring properties.

Phoebe knocked on the door, which opened a crack. She looked at it.

"Hello?" she called, "hello Mrs Walker?"

Heavy footsteps rushed up the hall, and she took a step back, just in time to give free rein for a teenage boy to storm out of the house.

She turned to watch him go as he turned, scowling, to flip the bird back at the house.

She heard slippers scuffing up the hall and turned back to the house.

"Greg," Mrs Walker called, "Greg wait. Your father didn't mean—"

Her voice cut out as she caught sight of Phoebe.

Greg paused for a moment as she asked, "Phoebe, what are you doing here?"

Greg nodded, as if she'd answered a question, and walked away down the sidewalk, throwing his backpack on his back.

"Greg," Mrs Walker called, raising her hand towards him, clearly caught between running after him and getting rid of Phoebe.

She sighed, and turned towards Phoebe, "how can I help you Miss Swan?"

"Don't mind me, if you need to go after your son, I can wait."

"Not at all, come inside."

She followed the woman's back down a long hall and through to a large combined kitchen-dining room that didn't seem to have been updated since the seventies, with brown mosaic tiles on the benches and orange florals on the floor.

Mr John Walker was sitting at a round table that was too small for the space.

"Can I make you a cup of tea Phoebe?"

"Just let her spit out what she came for," he growled.

Phoebe didn't remember him being quite this aggressive during her Police enquiries. "Do you mind if I sit down?" she asked pointedly.

John, clearly still annoyed by his son's departure, kicked a chair out from under the table.

Phoebe decided in that moment not to mention that the dead girl wasn't Lette.

Or that there was any hint of anything odd about the autopsy.

But she had to be subtle about it.

"Lette's remains are with the Victorian Institute of Forensic Medicine, and they're about to redo the autopsy."

"Why the hell would they do that," John asked.

"Is that not what you had her exhumed for?"

He glared at his wife. There was definitely something going on between them, but Phoebe couldn't guess what it was.

She made a mental note to follow up on what exactly John Walker had been doing when Lette was kidnapped, and since then

After a pause, where no one said anything, Phoebe continued.

"Not to worry, the initial autopsy was cursory, and as the progress of forensic science has been remarkable in the last few years, there may be additional information that comes to light this time.

"Can you tell me anything further about the last day you saw Lette?"

"We told you all about that at the time."

"That isn't exactly how I would describe it, Mr Walker," she consulted her notes, "you said you had dropped her off at her fish and chip shop job about seven o'clock, and when you went back for her at 11, she had left to walk home. You followed the most likely route, but didn't see her."

"Sounds about right."

"Why would your sixteen-year-old daughter start walking home Mr Walker, "wouldn't she have waited for you?"

"I don't remember."

"I think you can Mr Walker, I think you can remember exactly what happened and choose not to tell me."

He stood up so abruptly his chair skittered across the floor, "I don't have to listen to this, I haven't done anything wrong," he said.

"Then why won't you tell me?"

He stalked out.

She turned to Mrs Walker, who had stopped just inside the room, wringing her hands.

"What about you Mrs Walker?"

"I don't know anything. I was at the supermarket stacking shelves from about five until about midnight. When I got home the house was dark and I assumed everyone was tucked up in bed."

"Are you telling me your husband had gone to bed when he knew your daughter was missing?"

"Well, they'd been fighting— I've said too much."

Phoebe made a mental note to follow up on her alibi as well.

"Fighting about what Mrs Walker?"

"Oh, you know the stuff. Hem to short, too make-up, going out with a hoodlum. John thought Lette was growing up too fast, and too wild."

That was the problem when you came to a case thinking it was one thing, and it turned out to be another one entirely.

"What about Greg?"

"Oh, he was only five years old at the time, change of life baby and all that. On a normal night, John would have stayed home to look after him, but I think he'd stayed over at a friend's house."

She'd already heard a lot that hadn't come out at the time.

Certainly a lot that needed to be corroborated.

"I think I have enough for now, but I'd hoped to get another DNA sample. If you don't have anything of Lette's anymore, I could a sample from both your husband and yourself."

John Walker came back into the kitchen at that point, "then you can take mine as long as you bugger off out of this house."

Phoebe took a swab from him, and his wife, and left the house.

Going back to her office via the VIFM for analysis.

Back in her grey cubicle at the Wilkinson's Collins Street office, she sorted through the file to see where she was up to.

The VIFM was looking at the body end of things.

She was about to investigate the family.

There was still the money to be found.

She was in two minds about whether to look into Mason, but there was no need to do it straight away. The most important thing was probably to look into the family first.

They married a couple of years before Lette was born, and bought the house that same year for $135,000. Taken out a second mortgage for the ransom, and the bank foreclosed shortly after.

They sold it for less than was owing.

John Walker had a relatively stable career, the last decade or so as a car salesman. No wonder he was highly irritable.

Prior to that...

He'd taken an apprenticeship in the Dahlia Funeral Home...

At the conclusion of his apprenticeship, he'd stayed on until they held his daughter's funeral.

And if the VIFM found the identity of the girl buried in Lette's place, Phoebe was prepared to wager the funeral had been one of the Dahlia Funeral Home's.

It was entirely possible that he'd had enough of the funeral industry after Lette died.

But it was equally possible that something had happened and they'd not only fired him, but blacklisted him throughout the industry.

She checked the business ownership; husband and wife team, transferring the business to their son. The names were familiar; the couple who owned the business, were the couple who'd bought the Walker's house.

They'd bought the house *after* he'd moved into car sales.

Were they good friends, or had there been some kind of blackmail or extortion incident? If she checked their banking records, would she find a deposit of $100,000; the money that was supposed to be paid to the kidnappers?

There was evidence of ongoing repayments to the bank, but no trace of rent payments, or perhaps repayments on an informal loan.

So, something to park, but not make any further enquiries until she could establish more information without approaching either couple.

Mrs Walker had an alibi; that she'd been working, so Phoebe's next step was to call the supermarket.

Happily, the woman who'd been her supervisor at the time was still working for the company, albeit in a different position.

Phoebe didn't hold out much hope of anything useful.

"Oh yes Miss Swan," she said, "I remember the night very well, because the thing about Lette was all over the news the next day. And Grace was definitely there that night.

"Except for her "lunch" break, she said she just had to run out for an errand. She was only supposed to be half an hour, but ended up taking a little over an hour."

So effectively Mrs Walker's alibi was shot.

She was clicking her fingernails on the surface of her desk, trying to work out what to look at next, when her phone rang.

Greg Walker was in the downstairs reception wanting to speak to her. She asked them to set up a small interview room for her and went down to see him.

He was around five years old when Lette went missing, so would he be able to offer anything concrete to her investigation?

Greg was a little nervous, looking around in case someone had followed him. She offered him a seat and he took it, but couldn't seem to settle.

She took the seat opposite him, "you asked to see me?"

"There's more to this than they're letting on," he said.

"Your parents?"

"Yes. They have strong religious beliefs, that's what we were arguing about. They want me to do something I don't want to do."

"Like stay home and study?"

"No, like go out and proselytise."

"Like the Witnesses or Scientologist?"

He made a sound of exasperation, "no. Like Charles Manson, or the People's Temple."

Phoebe sat up and regarded him steadily. He returned her gaze, with the right amount of eye contact. His breathing was even, and his voice steady. "You think they did something to Lette?"

"She was afraid of them. They didn't like that she was seeing an outsider—

"I mean I say outsider, but I mean someone outside the group. She'd been promised to a boy in the group a few years older than her when she was a child, and she was to be sent to him on her sixteenth birthday."

"Do you think that's where she is?" Phoebe asked.

"No. I think they killed her because she wanted to leave the church."

"That's a little extreme don't you think?"

He sighed and scrubbed his face with both hands. "They signed a contract, and there were penalties for not passing her over."

"But the legal age of marriage is 18."

"They'd gone to court, arguing exceptional and unusual circumstances, and a magistrate made the Order."

"What were the circumstances?"

"I don't know, I was only a child. Can't you look it up?"

"I can, I just wondered if you knew. When do you think they killed her?"

"The night she was," he held his fingers up, gesturing air quotes, "'kidnapped', they sent me to my friend's house to sleepover." He slumped in his chair, "I didn't have a clue what they were up to or I would have warned her.

"I should have warned her."

Phoebe did not reach out to pat his hand, "you did the best you could."

He pulled a tissue from his pocket and blew his nose.

"Now it's my turn. They've arranged a marriage for me, and I don't want any part of it. I've got a flight to Sydney this afternoon, and after that, I'm not saying what my plans are.

"But if I turn up dead, it's because of them."

"Is there anything I can do to help," Phoebe asked, but she bloody hoped not.

"Nah," he said with a faint smile, "you need to stay clear of this one. I can take care of myself."

He stood up, and picked up his backpack, "I'll be off now, I've done what I came to do. I hope wherever she is, Lette can forgive me."

Phoebe extended her hand, "then I wish you good luck. And if you ever need to find me, well, you know where I am."

《《 • 》》

Phoebe called Jane and arranged to meet her the next day.

"We now know the identity of our dead girl; Serena Hoskins."

"And was the funeral held by Dahlia Funeral Home?"

Jane consulted her notes, "how did you know?"

"John Walker, Lette's father worked there."

"Funny you should say that. I had Serena's remains sampled, and the DNA is a match to Grace Walker, but John Walker is not the father."

"That is insane!" Phoebe said.

"I know."

"The Walkers were apparently in a cult, and their son thinks they may have been responsible for Lette's murder."

"I can't believe that. In this day and age?"

"So, we've figured out who the bodies are, a possible motive, and probably where the money went.

I think it's time to turn the evidence over to the Police."

Phoebe was at the Walker's house the day the Police came to arrest them.

"I knew you would work it out," Mrs Walker said as they handcuffed her, "the guilt has been eating me alive."

Phoebe didn't say anything, just closed the door behind her.

A few days later, a postcard featuring a picture of a large basket of roses arrived at the office.

"Good job," it said.

THE END

Derek Ericsson slumped at his desk, situated in the centre of a sea of grey cubicles in the northeast quadrant of the floor his soulless, heartless employer occupied.

Furthest from the convenience of the toilets, and the kitchens, but not far enough from the aromas drifting through the ventilation shafts.

Derek was in his forties, his balding pate inadequately concealed by his comb-over, with not nearly enough courage to shave his head and be done with it.

It was after six, and there was next to no one left in the office. He risked ducking down behind his desk to take a shot of vodka from the water bottle he'd decanted it into, and popped a mint in his mouth on the way up.

His bitch of a thirty-something overachieving boss would sack him on the spot if she knew about the day drinking.

And then he would be forced to stay home with his demon spawn children. Lucy aged three, T—

and Peter aged twelve.

As usual, he winced as he almost named Thomas. Beautiful, angelic Tommy who would have been ten this year, had he not been mown down on the sidewalk outside their home by a drunk driver when he was six.

Derek was haunted by the nameless, faceless driver who had never been found.

Lucy was his wife's replacement child.

Somehow, she'd moved on, leaving him behind.

But he just couldn't get past Tommy, the light of his life, now cold and alone in death.

"Derek, Derek, Derek," she who shall remain nameless dropped down to his level in a cloud of some kind of musky perfume.

"What am I going to do with you?"

Derek slumped even lower, the picture of misery.

She put her palm on his shoulder and pushed him upright, "you know Wilkinson's won't stand for this."

He refused to meet her eyes or say anything.

"Derek," she shook his shoulder, "look, I like you. You're reliable, and the best analyst in my team. I would hate to lose you."

He risked looking up at her, to see her face full of compassion.

A tear leaked from his eye and fell on her knee.

She shook his shoulder again, gentler this time, "you have to get your shit together. I won't be able to hide it forever."

Another tear dropped, though his face remained passive and still.

"Take a month off. See someone."

She stepped away and he heard her rummaging through a draw in her desk by the window.

In a few moments, she was back, pressing a crumpled business card into his hand, "see her. She'll help. Now go."

He dropped the card in his pocket without looking at it and scrambled to pick up his briefcase and leave before she changed her mind.

He risked looking back at the door as he left, "call her," she shouted, "I'll let her know to expect your call."

And then he scuttled away as fast as he could.

《《 • 》》

Shirley Weaving, Private Investigator was at that moment enjoying an animated debate with Great Uncle Edward Weaving, her spirit guide about the relative merits of the old or new Magnum, and therefore which one to watch that evening.

Obviously, there was a clear divide between the living and the dead. They needed a circuit breaker, but then again, they often did.

Great Uncle Edward had insisted she take the old heritage-listed building with the grand façade, in a leafy main street of an older, well established south-eastern suburb of Melbourne.

It was one of 25 shops running around the corner, along two sides of a large park.

Originally, shops had lined both streets, but these were all that remained, with larger modern constructions replacing the old before the heritage listing came through.

She, on the other hand, had been keen on the stark, ultra-modern office with the hip inner-city location.

But, she had to agree the location he'd chosen was delightful.

Her shop sat opposite the statue and garden commemorating the war dead, with a view through to the local sports ground.

The balcony of the flat above the shop had a good view of community activities all year round.

The shop front had beautiful stained-glass panels along the top, bottom and sides of the full-length picture windows. The wooden floorboards creaked reassuringly as she walked on them.

And her collection of random second-hand furniture collected from rubbish dumps and council collections somehow looked satisfyingly right in situ.

There was an excellent Chinese restaurant at one end of one leg, the post office at the other, and a magnificent bakery more or less in the middle. Not to mention a delicious café, small continental butcher, and an organic produce store. All the necessities of life nearby.

Within a five-minute walk of the tram terminus, and twenty minutes from the train station.

It was entirely possible Great Uncle Edward preferred this location as there was a "better" quality of ghost neighbours than the inner-city-working-class location.

The elderly owner died shortly after she moved in, and conveniently, the estate gave her the option to purchase the freehold.

She hated to say he was right, but she had to admit there was something slow and satisfying about the location, and her particular line of detective services flourished here.

Not that she made a big deal about that.

The day had been one of those slow days, the kind she usually associated with the calm before the storm. As if some beneficent entity gave her a quiet day to build her strength.

She'd caught up with all her filing, sent reminders for the overdue accounts, and in a burst of vanity, even cleaned the brass business plaque fixed on the pillar beside the door.

All the outstanding activities were taken care of, and there was nothing left to do.

She'd gratefully closed and locked the door, and climbed the wooden stairs to her apartment come storage unit above the office.

Once there, she opened a bottle of Cabernet Sauvignon, microwaved some leftover Chinese and opened a dialogue about whether to watch the old or new *Magnum P.I.*.

Edward had to be convinced, if not, he simply cut the power. As he'd done with *John Wick*, claiming it wasn't suitable viewing for a young woman.

She'd been forced to watch it at her friend Gabrielle's place and had conveniently forgotten the small brick fragment she generally carried to permit him to visit locations with her.

"Someone's coming," he said, breaking into her point of Magnum proof.

She dropped her hand, letting the remote fall to the floor as she turned to look towards the window overlooking the park.

Not that she could see the street from the flat upstairs, but she could feel a tangled mess of black, orange and red moving along the side-walk toward her. Its cold, sucking energy seemed to draw her in, and Edward put his hand on her shoulder to hold her steady.

"Whatever that is," she said, "is like a black hole sucking all the life and energy of everything around it into itself."

He grunted in agreement, "perhaps some kind of grief eating monster."

She snapped her fingers, and a halo of gold-tipped white and yellow sprang up around her.

"It's right outside the shop," he said, gripping her shoulder more firmly.

They watched it looking in the office for a while before it turned and walked back the way it had come.

She let the halo dissipate and flopped onto the couch, "I'm exhausted!"

Edward sat beside her and grunted in agreement, "I wonder if that was the Ericsson guy Gabrielle called about."

"I'd say so. She said we'd know what to do when he got here."

"Some kind of exorcism?"

"Well," she let out a sigh, "I can already tell there's some massive thing eating away at him, but until we meet him, I won't know what it's going to take to strip it away."

"No...

"I think maybe I might need to ask around my fellow guides..."

She took advantage of his preoccupation to start watching the new Magnum. When he realised, the lights started flickering, but then he subsided to the couch and enjoy the show.

The next morning, she prepared for the visit of the owner of the black aura by burning clove oil to purify the space, calm the owner and enhance her gifts.

She filled up the coffee machine ready to go, put the kettle on in case he wanted tea, and opened a fresh packet of chocolate biscuits.

As part of her preparation routine, she put on *Never Mind the Bollocks, Here's the Sex Pistols*, and jacked up the volume. Jumping, headbanging and dancing to dissipate the stress and tension that had been building since the visitation last night.

And to prevent it from getting worse.

What could the owner of such negative vibes need with her services?

Shirley was a fully licensed Private Investigator, and did all the usual kind of investigations; background checks, computer and phone forensics, missing persons, surveillance.

It was just, well, she had outside help.

So far out, it was from the Other Side.

From Great Uncle Edward.

Who added an unearthly dimension to the investigations.

She felt it approaching again and allowed the fear to shift her perception a little higher, before turning to look out the window.

Without her third eye, she would have seen a perfectly ordinary white, middle-aged man. Receding hairline, expanding waistline, bowed and exhausted by the weight of something.

With her third eye, she could see the monster he was carrying on his back. An awful, ugly, bloated monster. It looked kind of like a diseased, bloated corpse, crossed with an insanely large slug whose rows of sharp teeth were firmly locked on his neck.

No wonder he looked kind of wasted and greyed out with the weight of the monster.

"I don't know why I'm here," he said as she opened the door for him.

A crackle of energy heralded the arrival of Edward, "what in the name of all that's holy is that thing?"

<I'm not sure,> she thought back.

As if the creature knew it was talking about it, it kind of twisted its head without moving and focused its small and beady eyes on them.

<What the fuck!> she thought.

"Indeed," Edward said, and after a short pause, as if he'd just realised, "language!"

"Why don't you come in and tell me about it," she said, taking a step back and indicating a translucent folding screen with an oriental pattern, behind which a couple of cosy chairs were visible, but obscured.

"Sure," he said and moved forward. He looked as though it was taking a lot of effort as if he was walking waist-deep through water.

She tried to keep her face impassive as the creature appeared to be trying to make him turn around and walk out again.

"Here sit down," she said, "would you like something to drink? Tea? Coffee? Water?"

The creature recoiled, as though something had poked it. It writhed around on the man's neck, and somehow, pulled itself inside the man's body.

It seemed the clove oil was working, though not exactly in the way she'd intended.

"Coffee please. I feel like I need the kick."

Edward turned the machine on, and the man turned to look at it.

"It's on a timer. Milk and sugar?"

"Milk and two sugars," he replied.

She'd previously noticed people relaxed when they watched a woman bustle in a kitchen, so she asked, "why don't you tell me what's bothering you while I make it?"

He slumped in an armchair and sank into himself.

"My name's Derek Ericsson."

Definitely Gabrielle's guy.

She knew the nub of the matter now, dead child, and it looked like the monster was feeding off Derek's grief.

Nonetheless, she made a questioning encouraging noise, as she walked to the kitchen where he watched her grab a couple of mugs from a wall cabinet.

She let him talk, occasionally encouraging him to continue as she put the biscuits on a plate and brought them over. And then returned with the coffee. And then sat down next to him.

"I'm guessing that you'd like me to find the driver of the car?"

"Yes," he said, the most decisive thing he'd said.

The creature lunged out of his neck, but as it met the clove oil suspended in the atmosphere, retreated again almost instantly.

"I will certainly do my best, but it's been four years, so I'm not sure what I'll be able to achieve."

Derek smiled. Just a small smile, but his face showed a tiny sign of hope.

"Thank you. I know there's a one in a million chance, but I just don't know where to start looking."

The creature popped its head out and glared at her.

"You've given me a location, and a date and time of death, and that's a start."

Derek pulled out of his slump, and sat straighter in the chair, "how will you move on?"

"I'm not sure exactly, probably start with the police report, talk to your wife and any witnesses."

"No one came forward at the time."

"Not to worry, sometimes things like this weigh on people, and after a while, they feel the need to unburden themselves."

He smiled a straight lipped smile, "I suppose they do. Look at me here, after all this time, trying to find out."

"Quite so. What will you do in the meantime?"

"I've been feeling tired and suicidal. As though I just can't take it anymore. But now, I feel like I can breathe at last. As though I've taken the first step towards something significant."

"Just hold onto that thought for a moment."

She went back to the cupboard under the stairs, "something for grief," she said, as if she was thinking.

Edward picked out a piece of raw obsidian.

She passed it through the haze of clove oil the burner was emitting, and brought it back to Derek.

"Take this piece of obsidian, and when you feel yourself sliding back, take it out and turn it around and around in your hand."

He took it, dropped it as if it was hot, and scrambled to find it and pick it up again. "I'm sorry, I don't know how it fell through my fingers!"

Shirley could see the creatures head coming out of Derek's neck as far as it dared, glaring at her. So, once he'd grabbed it again, she reached out and folded her hands around his.

"It's going to be okay. We're going to get through this."

He smiled hesitantly, and she could see a small piece of him was ready to return to living. He let his hands stay in hers for a moment, and then put the stone in his pocket and stood up.

"Shall I call back next week to see how it's going?"

"Of course. I'll definitely have something for then."

She took a step back freeing the path towards the door, not wanting to get any closer to the monster.

Derek left, standing a little taller and free-er than when he'd arrived. He paused at the door, the creature struggling to expand beyond his body again, but left without saying another word.

The first step was to call her friend Jeremy, at the Department of Justice about the Police case file.

"You know I can't just look up the system - it tracks all the access requests against the Freedom of Information file numbers. But if the case is still unsolved after four years, chances are it's available.

"Send me the FOI request and I'll get onto it straight away."

The next step was to take Edward with her to look at the crime scene.

It was one of the newer subdivisions, with roundabouts and other traffic calming devices. Given the address, she could see the driver must have driven straight over the roundabout and mounted the curb on the other side.

By the look of it, the incident could have been a lot worse. The house was at the minimum distance from the kerb, and without a fence they were lucky.

The car could have taken out the kid, and half the front of the house as well.

<Are there any entities around here?> she asked him telepathically.

"Nothing obvious," he said, "but there's something here. I suppose you can feel it.

<Definitely something,> she rotated on the spot, looking in all directions. She felt itchy, like every millimetre of skin was bitten by mosquitoes.

<Feels like it's coming from across the road,> she scratched her arm.

"Mmm."

She rotated to the right, a bit to the left, and then right again until she was looking at an undeveloped two-story house within a garden consisting of builder's rubble.

A curtain twitched.

Edward was over there in an instant, "there's a woman here, she has one of those worm things attached to her neck."

<I'll be there in a sec,> she said, applying some clove oil diluted with unscented hand cream to her hands and arms as she strolled over to the house.

She knocked on the door, and nothing happened within the house.

"She won't answer," Shirley turned to see a plump, middle-aged woman hanging over the fence.

"Why not?"

"Her daughter died about four years ago."

Shirley turned toward Edward standing by the front door; he shrugged his shoulders.

"Yes," the woman continued, "just after they moved in. Leukaemia it was. Poor Mrs Andrews never got over it."

Shirley turned back towards the woman, "actually, I'm a private investigator hired by Mr Ericsson to look into his son's death," she pulled out her license for the woman to check. "Did the Andrew's girl die around the same time?"

The woman looked at the card, thought for a while, then handed it back. "Yes, it was around the same time. June that year was a really bad month.

"And as well as those two kids, there was the Jackson girl at number 22 from an accident at the recreational centre, the Lee boy at 23 drowned in their swimming pool, and Miss Dine's new puppy at 24.

"Bit Mr Singh at number 25 and had to be put down. I don't think they've spoken to each other since then."

Edward appeared behind the woman, giving Shirley a hard look.

"So, six houses clustered close by," she said, looking back at him, "that's dreadful! Surely not all on the same day?"

"Oh no, pretty much the same as I said. Ericsson was first, the next day the Andrews' girl, the next day Jackson, then Lee, then the puppy incident, then the puppy was euthanised."

"Five deaths in six days? That doesn't make sense."

"No-no, five deaths in five days. Now that I think about it, that's quite shocking. I suppose that's the benefit of time."

There was something nudging at the back of Shirley's mind, and she couldn't tell whether keeping the woman talking would spill it over into her consciousness and send it further away.

"Were you here the day Thomas Ericsson died?"

"Oh yes, I run the local childcare co-op, so I'm always here. I didn't see the accident, but I heard the thud. Someone started screaming, and the car backed up and drove away. Miracle the car started."

"They found what was left of it on the vacant ground for the new subdivision in Charles Street. Burnt out wreck apparently. They just towed the car away and started the construction." The woman shuddered luxuriously, "I wouldn't want to be living in that house I can tell you."

"So you didn't see anything?"

"No one saw anything. Considering the screaming, it was so strange. No one saw anything when
any of the children died. It was like some kind of
demonic intervention." She shuddered again.

The sound of children screaming came from inside the house.

"I'd best be getting back," she said, turning away,
"good luck with your investigations. That family
could really do with some good luck."

<I'm getting the feeling there should be more
deaths,> she thought to Edward.

"I feel like there should be at least another two."

<Do you think all the families have these things
in their necks?>

"Grief slugs? We're two for two with Mrs Andrews."

<Should we check the other families?>

"Yes. I really think we should."

Shirley paused to put more clove oil hand cream
on her hands and arms, then walked to the next
house in the street.

They visited numbers 22 through to 25, ostensi-
bly searching for evidence to do with the Ericsson
matter, but really looking for more evidence of grief
slugs.

And they found it in all the houses except Derek Ericsson's

"Oh, I made him move out a couple of years ago," Mrs Ericsson said, "he was bringing the whole family down with his relentless Tommy this and Tommy that."

Edward gave her a hard look.

"I'm sorry if this seems insensitive," Shirley said, "but weren't you affected by Thomas' death?"

Mrs Ericsson sighed. "Yes. It was very hard at the time.

"But my son, Peter was hurting just as much, if not more than Derek, and he just couldn't see it. I didn't want Peter's life to be overshadowed by Thomas' death.

"And then Lucy came along, and I didn't have the time to dwell on Thomas anymore. Lucy deserved two fully functioning parents, but one was better than none.

"Actually, it was Thomas' birthday the other day, and we went to the cemetery to visit him."

"I see," Shirley replied.

What was it about Derek that the grief slug could overwhelm his defences when his wife and son could fight it off?

"Why do you think he couldn't move on from the death of his son?" she asked

Mrs Ericsson thought about it for a while, "because he's always gone all-in on everything - it's his nature to overachieve. Though I couldn't say where it came from."

"I see."

"Look, I'd love to chat more; there's something about you that makes it easy, but the kids will be home soon, and I need to get ready.

"Tell Derek to get his shit together, and come back home to where he belongs."

"I will," Shirley said, and watched the woman walk away.

You couldn't get more of a contrast between the two of them. She was fit and vibrant, he was anything but. She was calm and confident, while he was bowed beneath the weight of the grief slug.

<We have to figure out where the grief slugs came from, and how to kill them.>

"I couldn't agree with you more."

Shirley walked back to the street and looked up and down.

<Could the slugs be something that was here already, or was it introduced?>

Edward shrugged, "beats me. Let's go home and do some research."

Back in the office, she mixed up some lemon, cypress and rosemary essential oils for focus and concentration, and lit the oil burner.

And he disappeared, presumably to check his spirit sources about the monster.

She sat on the couch, crossed her legs, and started researching slugs on her laptop. Not that she knew it was a slug, but it was somewhere to start.

Before long, she'd uncovered two possible methods of transfer.

Some slugs transmit genetic material through darts they fire at other slugs.

Other slugs leave clutches of up to 30 eggs deposited somewhere damp, like under a rock or log. Where they lay dormant until the conditions are right for them to hatch.

To be honest, the dart was her favourite, but given most parasites breed in the soil and are transmitted by skin contact, it seemed more likely that was the method of transfer.

So.

As a new subdivision, it was possible a grief slug egg cache was already there, ready to be disturbed during the construction phase.

But it was more or less equally possible, some kind of carrier had visited each of the houses on subsequent days. Someone like a council inspector certifying occupancy.

Ah, but it was after they moved in, so not the council. Could the builder have sent someone to catalogue or fix construction faults?

She needed to know more about the car that killed the Ericsson boy.

In a rare moment of synchronicity, the phone rang. She pulled it out of her pocket; it was Jeremy.

"I'll post the documents out to you, but the vehicle was registered to Jeff Dawson, who claimed it had been stolen the night before. Guess who he worked for?"

"Would it be QPY Construction?"

"Oh my god! Every time! Post-construction follow up."

She laughed, "I was out at the site investigating this morning."

"Ah. Well, I bet you can't guess what happened to Jeff Dawson after the crash."

"He died?"

"Again? Bet you don't know how."

"I don't, but I'd be interested to find out."

"Suicide. It seems his wife and child were hit by a train a year or so before the Ericsson case, and he hadn't got over it."

Edward reappeared in the office and started talking.

"Shhh-it," she said, making a quelling motion, "he suicided? How?"

"Crashed his car. Is it possible he decided spur of the moment to drive headfirst into the Ericsson house, not realising the boy was right in front of him?"

"Crashed his car?" she said looking at Edward, who nodded, "I imagine it's possible. Likely even. What did the Police report say?"

"They didn't interview him; he died the day before they contacted him. That's why the investigation closed - couldn't prove it either way."

"Thanks so much Jeremy, I owe you."

"Sure do, what about some of those strudels with the extra cloves?"

"Next time you're here?"

"It's a date. Then you can tell me all about your case."

"Sure thing. I'll see ya."

"Not if I see ya first," he cackled, and hung up before she could get a comment in.

She threw the phone down, stood up and stretched, "I have so much to tell you," she said to Edward.

"And I you, but you go first."

She filled him in on slug reproduction, including the dart method. Then about the driver visiting each of the houses and potentially transmitting the slugs.

And then her theory, that if they didn't get rid of the Ericsson slug, it would drive him to suicide shortly.

"Well, he did mention it was all getting too much for him, and he wished he was dead," Edward said.

"Al least we can tell him who was responsible for his son's death to put his mind at ease. But if we can't kill the slug, I think it will kill him. And presumably send out slug darts to those in the vicinity as it dies."

"Yes," Edward said. "What about the cloves - the oil in the burner made it pull itself back into Ericsson's body. Can you administer it orally?"

"Actually yes. Jeremy was asking for some apple strudel. I could make a batch with too many cloves in it. That ought to be enough to drive it out of Ericsson's body."

"So sweet," said Edward, making a heart shape with his fingers and resting his chin on them.

Shirley made a face at him, "all that's left then, is figuring out a way of killing the grief slug when it's exposed. Something easily transferable to the other families."

"Interesting conundrum," said Edward, "how do you kill a creature no one can see?

"I don't know much about grief slugs *per se*, but you can kill ordinary slugs with coffee, beer, vinegar, cornmeal, ammonia, garlic, ash, and copper."

"Or is there some kind of bird or frog-like monster predator or slug parasite we could use?"

"Chickens love slugs. And chickens have ultraviolet vision, so it's possible they could see the slugs."

"You know who has chickens?" Shirley asked, "the Singh's have chickens. That might be why Mr Singh didn't catch the slugs. I wonder if they'd let us borrow one?"

"No need, Edna a couple of doors down has some."

"Right," said Shirley, counting on her fingers, "apple strudel to drive it out, and a chicken to kill it. Shall we call Ericsson?"

"I think sooner is better than later, but what if we can't contain the monster?"

"You raise a valid point, but I don't think we can afford to wait. We could try a mix of patchouli and bergamot to relax the emotion centres and promote emotional balance."

"Okay, let's do it. Though I don't know that I can do anything to protect you if this goes wrong."

"We'll worry about that later."

She called him, and he agreed to visit the next day.

The next day, she made their preparations; the oils in the burner, the coffee and strudel, the Sex Pistols, and the chicken, contained in a pen with a handful of corn.

When Derek arrived, she was waiting with the coffee and strudel.

The slug seemed smaller, and he seemed less bent and more capable, so she guessed he'd turned a corner.

He tucked into his snack as they talked about the weather and other inconsequentialities.

The slug wasn't happy, roiling on his neck as though it had a stomach ache. Not too much; it seemed the oils were doing a good job of anaesthetising it.

Suddenly the chicken broke through its pen and made a rush at the slug, leaping through the air and scratching it off Derek's neck in passing.

He brushed his neck, not noticing the blood, watching in fascination as the bird appeared to be rolling on its back and shaking its head like a cat with a toy.

"Is your chicken okay? It seems to be having a fit."

"I'm sure it's fine. I hope it's fine. I'm looking after it for a friend." And before too long, it had eaten the slug all up, and was sitting grooming its feathers as if nothing had happened.

"Oh look, you've scratched your neck," Shirley said, "let me dress it for you."

So far as she could tell, the wound was clean, "this will sting a little," she said dabbing some alcohol on it, then adding a dressing.

Fingers crossed it would be fine.

He watched the bird, as she shared the information she'd discovered, while she watched him, looking for any evidence something of the slug had remained behind.

"How do you feel?" she asked when she'd finished.

Derek frowned, "I'm a bit sad about the guy driving the car. The death of his wife and child must have been eating away at him, and I know how that feels."

She made an encouraging noise.

"But I feel like I've wasted the last few years. My kids are strangers to me now, and it'll take some work to regain their trust.

"But I know it will be worth it. And thanks to you, my wife will welcome me back. And my boss too."

"I'm glad," she said.

It seemed safe to let him go.

The next day, she and Edward visited the other houses with grief slug infestations, taking the strudel and the chicken with them.

One by one, they watched the slug disarmed by the strudel, and dismembered by the chicken.

All in all, an exhausting yet satisfying day.

《《 • 》》

They sat on the balcony, enjoying a well-earned beer and watching the neighbourhood kids playing five-a-side soccer on the green.

"Good job Edward," she said, raising her glass to him.

"Good job Shirley," replied, raising his to her.

"Hope we never see those grief slugs again."

He shuddered delicately, "bloody hope not too."

One of the teams in the park scored a goal, and cheered and jumped and hugged each other.

"I was thinking Chinese to celebrate," she said.

"Don't you dare make any chicken jokes."

"Not Kung Pao?"

"No.

"Not General Tso's?

"No."

"Not Moo Goo Gai?"

"No."

"I've had enough of you and chicken for one day," he stood up, "I'm off."

She smiled, "see you tomorrow then," she said as he winked out.

An hour later, Jeremy arrived with more beer.

"Are you alone?" he asked, looking wildly about the room as if expecting a bogey man.

"He's gone. We're good. Did you bring the CD?"

He looked around, then pulled three out of his backpack. "*Invasion of the Body Snatchers*; 1956, 1978, and that weird 2007 version."

"Perfect. I got take out. Come upstairs where we can watch them in comfort."

They snuggled up on the couch as he queued the 1956 version.

"So, how was your day?" she asked

"Nothing much. You?"

"Same."

It was nice to take a break from the surreal now and again, but she wouldn't want to live there.

THE END

Susan stifled a yawn into her shoulder and rolled her eyes at Ryan, the colleague she was usually paired up with.

The briefing meeting was the boring as bat shit calm before the storm.

Mimma, their boss, had collected together the four teams who'd be primarily responsible for surveillance of Nick Liang.

She's been talking for an hour already, with the accompanying slide presentation detailing the information the background team had collected, and what the executive committee hoped they could achieve with additional surveillance.

"Our client has alleged Liang is the head of the criminal organisation who killed her son himself. Your job is to document every place he goes and every person he sees."

"Isn't that a job for the Police?" Ryan asked.

"Our client has not received satisfaction from the Police, and has engaged us to collect the necessary evidence.

"Any further questions?

"Then you have the weekend to yourselves and will commence this operation at 00:00 midnight Monday morning. It will run for one week, ending at 23:59 Sunday night.

"You are dismissed," she said and exited the meeting.

Susan stretched as she allowed the other attendees to leave the room. Why she'd ever thought working for the Wilkinson National Detective Agency (est. 1889), would be glamorous was beyond her.

The Collins Street offices were pretty nice, but she was rarely in them. More often than not she was outdoors, watching, trying not to be seen by others.

At least it was Summer, and it would be warm outside.

Susan stretched, closed her eyes, and turned to the sun hoping for a little extra oomph to recharge.

Not that there was much in the way of direct sun in the Bourke Street mall during the afternoon, but the rays reflecting from the shop windows would have to do.

According to her watch, there was a little over an hour until she clocked off, and if she was honest, she was exhausted.

Could not wait to hand over, and go home to a hot, spring blossom scented bath in her tiny bath, a glass of wine, and a Chinese take-out.

Quite possibly all at the same time while she listened to some smooth jazz, Norah Jones perhaps.

Not that her job was difficult *per se*, but following someone around, trying not to be conspicuous *was* quite tiring.

Which was why she always went nondescript for work; beige sundress, natural sandals, tortoiseshell sunglasses (not too big or small), no make-up, mouse-brown hair loosely tied in a ponytail at the back of her neck.

Absolutely nothing that might distinguish her during a casual scan of the crowd.

Except, for the keenly observant, she was almost always drawing in a sketch pad; her preferred way to keep track of the locations those she was tailing visited, and the people they met there.

Part life drawing, part Method of Loci memory palace for remembering details of interactions.

When pressed, as she had been once or twice, she would contend the mark was the most "unconventionally" attractive person she'd seen, and that was why she'd been following them.

Generally, the mark would call her a freak or a stalker, and tell her to leave; not necessarily quietly or politely.

Which she did, because the Agency always had teams of at least two people tailing the subjects of its investigations for just that reason.

It was a strategy that always worked, except *that* day.

She dropped her arms, and rolled her head backwards and forwards on her neck to ease the tension, and as she did, someone snatched the sketchbook from her lap.

She stood up, her eyes flicking open, ready to attack (in the nicest, most nondescript way) the person who'd taken the book.

Except.

It was the guy hanging out with the target.

She'd been made!

For a moment she was frozen, and it was just enough time for him to dance away, over the tram tracks with the book, flicking rapidly through the pages.

"I think she likes you," he called out to Nick, who looked amused because of course, everyone liked him.

And why wouldn't you when he wore a tight black t-shirt with black jeans and short black boots? When his shoulder-length dark hair shone with good health, and probably a lot of product too.

To go with the occasional glimpses of the silver stud in his ear and the heavy Bali silver chain he wore around his neck.

Following him around had been like watching an Asian drama live and in person. Everywhere he went, from café to market to supermarket people stopped to talk to him, and sometimes asked to have their photo taken with him.

If she didn't know better, she'd think he was an actor or something, knee-deep in admirers.

And that stupid guy was always with him. Though she'd only drawn one picture of him because he wasn't the target, and in about a millisecond that was going to get *really* embarrassing.

How the hell was she going to get out of this?

She couldn't leave the book with them; she hadn't remembered where he'd been, or who he'd been with. She hadn't needed to; it was all sketched out and she didn't need to remember it.

Not that the book identified her as a licensed private investigator, though she was required to carry her license when she was on the job.

But it did have her name, mobile phone number, and the post office box address of the Agency.

"Hey, these are pretty good," the guy said, showing them to Nick.

Oh my god, it just got worse and worse. This was going to be her off the case.

"Well, Susan Murray," said Nick, "can I buy you a drink?" as he started walking towards her.

Goddammit, she thought.

"Oh! No. I wouldn't dream of..."

Gak, try again, "I'm really not..."

Fuck's sake. "Just give me the book and I'll be on my way."

She took a step back as he and his cologne reached her, enveloping her in the smell of rainforest.

His hair fell down over his right eye as he smiled down at her, his warm brown eye meeting hers, looking every inch the cunning fist-fighting villain, the client suspected he was.

He smoothed a lock of hair that had escaped from her ponytail back, tucking it behind her ear.

Move, she thought-shouted at herself, don't stand here like a rabbit stuck in the oncoming car headlights!

He held his hand out behind him, and the other guy dropped the sketchbook in it, "you can only have it back if you let me buy you a drink."

She looked up at Nick, unable to break his gaze, weighing up the loss of a day's work with forcing her feet to turn around and walk away.

Stupid, stupid, stupid, she told herself.

He waggled the book, and she looked at it, and through it to Ryan on the other side of the mall.

She made a seemingly random coded gesture to tell him her cover was blown, and he nodded.

She looked back up at Nick and said, with bad grace "fine."

He smiled triumphantly, and grabbing her wrist, hustled her into a tiny restaurant tucked behind what used to be the main post office on the corner and was now a shopping arcade.

He ushered her into a booth and sat beside her, way too close.

Just when she thought she was on her own with him, and could maybe manage him, his friend sat opposite.

Not that he was any comfort, having got her into this mess he was unlikely to do anything to get her out of it.

In fact, it seemed to her that they had some kind of bet riding on whether he could get her to do… What?

Kiss him?

Sleep with him?

Take him back to her place?

Nick ordered wine and something to eat, not bothering to ask what she wanted.

He put the book on the table, and she made a grab for it.

"Ah ah ah-aa," he said, "not until you tell me why you were following us."

Good, she was prepared for that, "I just liked the way you moved," she shrugged, dipping her head as he quirked an eyebrow at his friend and slung his left arm along the back of the booth, and coincidentally around her.

Like a teenager at the movies.

She continued, "it's all kind of sharp and angled. Like a stick-insect transformed into human form."

He smiled a small smile, as if she'd said something amusing, and then opened the book, carefully turning the pages, smoothing his fingers over himself on the page.

"I don't see anything sharp or angled about these drawings, I see the grace and form of a ballet dancer."

A curious way to describe himself.

"Ballet dancer? Really?" she attempted to pull the book across again, but he held it steady, resting his right forearm on it.

"You can't fool me," he said, "these pictures are not of an insect, but someone you're teetering on the edge of falling in love with."

Okay, that part was true.

She'd been following him around for a couple of days and hadn't seen anything that would suggest he was the kind of guy the client thought he was.

All she'd seen, was Nick being courteous and wildly charming.

His head leaned toward her, almost touching, and spoke quietly "did you think I wouldn't notice a woman as beautiful as you in a crowd?"

She lifted her head so rapidly it connected with his, his stubble grazing her temple.

Her cover had definitely been blown. Maybe as early as the first day.

And if he'd spotted her, he'd probably changed his pattern, and there wasn't anything she'd drawn that was compromising. Or in any way reliable.

Except perhaps his likeness.

And maybe his friend's.

It was time to extract herself and disappear before his suspicions were roused. If they weren't already.

And hopefully, the guys on the other shifts would get whatever evidence they needed.

Because as it turned out, she had nothing.

She stood up abruptly, "I have to go."

Nick leaned towards the table, blocking her path, "but we've only just got here."

"I forgot; I have somewhere I need to be."

"Not another man I hope? Though your sketchbook only captures me and Ares here," he nodded his head toward Ares, who grinned wolfishly.

And too late, she started to get worried she was in over her head. She held her handbag to her chest like a shield, looking around, trying to spot any other Wilkinson agents.

But she didn't see anyone she knew; from the Agency or otherwise.

Had they planned this? Had they stacked the restaurant?

Or even worse, had they infiltrated the Agency?

Was it possible she'd been placed there because someone thought she'd be relatively easy to crack?

Or disposable?

"No, I—"

As her sense of panic mounted, she realised she was hyperventilating and tried to slow her breathing.

"It's none of your business. You can keep the sketchbook."

She was prepared to climb over him if she had to, but at the last moment, he subsided, dropping his arm and pushing himself back towards the seat so she could scramble past.

And she fled, running out of the restaurant, not looking back and catching the nearest tram. Fortunately going in her direction.

After a few stops, she got off that tram, and onto the next one that arrived.

And a few stops after that, changed again.

Then walked for about twenty minutes to be sure no one was following her, but also to get to a tram stop where she could catch a tram that would take her home.

Sadly, her desire to relax in a hot bath had dissipated; she felt twitchy between her shoulder blades. Though she was fairly confident no one was following her.

But, she got off the tram a few stops earlier than usual and stopped in a busy restaurant. She managed to get a partially concealed table in a corner where she had a good view of the door.

She ordered a few dishes to make it look like she was waiting for someone, and a bottle of wine. She drank a glass and nibbled at the dishes, looking around as if she was expecting someone.

Which she kind of was, but had no idea how she would know them. Except that they'd probably take a seat facing the door like her.

About an hour and a half later she'd drunk all the wine, eaten a significant amount of food, and felt safe enough to walk the rest of the home without looking behind her.

That didn't stop her looking from the corner of her eyes at the streetscape reflected in the closed, darkened shops as she walked down the high street.

Gradually passing from shops and businesses to flats and houses, with less passing traffic.

Trying to move with her usual confident stride.

She hadn't expected to be out late, and hadn't brought a light cardigan, so she shivered a little in the cool evening air.

As she turned off the high street, she ran the last couple of blocks to her block of flats, dancing in the few seconds it took for her security code to register.

A quick glance back at the street, and she fled up the stairs, hoping no one would see which floor she lived on.

Back in her one and a half room flat, she crawled across the floor to avoid anyone seeing her from the street, and closed the curtains before she let herself relax a little.

Then she rang Wilkinson's and talked to the evening duty manager. She quickly outlined that her cover had been blown, and she was a little concerned Nick had the opportunity to discover who she was, where she worked, and where she lived.

"Don't worry," she was told, "we'll have someone drive by your flat a couple of times during the night. Stay home tomorrow morning and wait for your duty supervisor to call you. If anything happens in the meantime, call in again."

She smiled to herself as she acknowledged she was probably overreacting, but she still waited for several long minutes before lighting a couple of candles rather than switching on the main overhead lights.

And tried not to worry that he'd already been through her flat, or had one of those devices that could see through walls.

She crept over to the fridge and drank some milk from the plastic bottle before crawling to the bedroom to strip her clothes off and rest.

And as she fell asleep, she wondered if she'd been mistaken.

Was it possible, the client had some kind of grudge against Nick?

That he wasn't a thieving gangster? That he was just misunderstood.

And then told herself to get a grip on herself.

Nick Liang might be pretty, but his reputation was ruthless.

She was pretty sure she'd read somewhere that he beat a guy to death with his bare hands. Over a girl, or a parking spot, or something he imagined.

No matter what, she couldn't get involved in any capacity with him because she was a private investigator who was investigating him.

It was such a massive conflict of interest it would jeopardise the veracity of her evidence and testimony.

And ruin her career as an investigator.

And with the stain of Nick Liang around her, any career she chose to take up once he'd got bored and dumped her.

Though potentially, that would give her the opportunity to try making a living from her art.

Call herself Banksia and refuse to make public appearances.

She sighed and thumped her pillows to try and make them more comfortable. Eventually, she fell asleep but slept fitfully.

The next morning, she could see the sun shining through the gaps in the curtains, in what looked to be another beautiful day.

Which was almost a shame as she'd drunk too much the night before, and the day seemed rather brighter than normal.

She dragged on the luxurious black and gold silk robe her mother gave her last Christmas and padded to what passed as a kitchen in her bare feet to put her coffee percolator on.

Reflexively, she relaxed into her morning routine as she heard it start heating up. The smell of the fresh grounds from the jar was almost enough to keep her going until it was done.

She drank a big glass of water, cut up some sour-dough and popped it in the toaster, got out some raw honey and cultured butter ready for when it popped.

On her way through to her tiny bathroom, she opened the curtains and windows.

And that was where the day started getting complicated because Nick Liang stood across the street, looking up.

She quickly took a step back away from the window, hoping he hadn't seen her, but afraid she couldn't be that lucky.

She rang her boss Mimma, and of course, the service diverted to the morning shift duty manager.

"Um, hi," she said. "It's Susan Murray from Day Surveillance Team five. I was assigned to watch Nick Liang last week, yesterday my cover was blown, and today he's right outside my house."

"I think I heard something about this in the briefing," she said, "please hold on," and before Susan could say another word, she was listening to an electric organ version of some kind of cheerful, never-ending pop music that she hoped wasn't the same "tune" the clients heard.

Her toast popped, which was a teensy bit inconvenient as she still hadn't been to the bathroom.

She put her mobile phone on speaker on the kitchen bench, and danced a bit while she buttered the toast, and added honey, then poured herself a black coffee with one teaspoon of sugar; knocking the spoon once against the side of the jar to even it up before it went into the cup.

Not really game to leave the phone, and not sure how long until the woman came back, she took it, and her breakfast, across to her dining table to eat.

Not that it was a dining table, more of a large coffee table in front of the couch.

And when she'd finished, continued to sit while she licked her index finger and picked the crumbs up with it.

Finally, a man picked up the call, "Susan, it's Ben Hall here."

She sucked her breath in, because he was the partner she nominally worked for.

Her big, big... big boss.

"Ah, hello Ben."

"Your, er, situation... has given us what you might call a unique opportunity. If you're willing."

"An opportunity?"

"Yes. If Nick Liang is interested in you, it's possible you may gain deeper access to his network than we currently have access to. The kind of access where we can gather more information to prove or disprove the client's hypothesis and get this investigation wrapped up quicker than expected."

"But—"

"Now there could be some danger in this activity, and we're prepared to make you an acting Level Four operative for the duration. How does that sound?"

"It sounds like a promotion, but I haven't undertaken any specialist training that would equip me for that kind of role."

"You don't have to do anything you're uncomfortable with, and you can quit the placement anytime."

The doorbell rang.

"I've got to go Ben, someone's at the door."

She opened the door, as Ben said, "think about it and let me know."

"I don't have a choice," she said, "he's right here at my door."

Nick cocked his head and looked pleased with himself.

"Okay then, I'll get a panic button brooch delivered to you today."

"Fine," she said and hung up.

Nick stepped over the threshold, and closed the door behind him "that's right, I'm here."

"What do you want Nick?"

He raised the sketchbook to eye level, "I brought your book back."

She reached for it, but he pulled it out of her reach.

"Didn't I say you had to have a drink with me to get it back?" he arched an eyebrow at her.

And honestly, he looked gorgeous when he did that, but she just wanted to push him back out the door again.

Maybe that was why he'd shut it.

She sighed and rubbed her forehead. It was so much easier in her beige dress, sketching him from across the street.

Next job, she was requisitioning a camera like everyone else.

"Didn't I tell you I picked you out of a crowd because you're so beautiful?"

"I don't recall you saying any such thing."

He reached out to lightly touch her robe, "so nice to see what you're really like; in *living* colour."

In one smooth movement, she turned away so he missed touching her, but the robe slid down her shoulder, reminding her she was naked underneath it.

And still hadn't visited the little girl's room.

Which raised another issue. Her flat was a small studio apartment. More or less all that kept her living and sleeping rooms apart were a Chinese style screen and a bead curtain.

Luckily the bathroom had a door.

And enough space to hung a small load of hand-washing to dry.

Unable to figure out how to get rid of him, she said "wait right *here*," and fled behind the screen.

Fortunately, in her line of work there was no room for "stage fright" - you might lose your target - so she got the bathroom thing out of the way lickedy-split.

She paused in front of the drying rack, thinking about what he'd said about living colour, and decided that if he wanted to get to know her, he would get to know the real her.

Not her quick disappear into a crowd work persona. It was about fine for eight hours of not being noticed, but as a woman of real, black and white opinions, hard to maintain.

Well, mostly the real her.

It would be dumb to let him get to know her.

She'd have to lie, and maybe when he found out about that, he'd back off. Fast.

She quickly dressed in mostly dry blue jeans and a red linen tunic.

When she got back to him, he wasn't *exactly* where she'd left him, but had taken two steps to the kitchen to make coffee for two.

Leaving her sketchbook on the table.

On the one hand annoying, but on the other, she *really* needed another coffee.

The doorbell rang, and he said, "I'll get that," almost sprinting to the door to his ubiquitous friend.

"Have you met Aresio?" Now that she looked at him, he would have seemed more attractive if he hadn't been standing next to Nick.

Funny that she hadn't really noticed him before; smooth blond hair, olive complexion, stunning blue eyes, with the same hidden, toned musculature. Something about him that seemed slightly menacing, now that she was giving him 100% of her focus.

But he wasn't the target, even if he was with him 95% of the time, and it was up to the analysts back in the office to identify and categorise him.

"Ares please," he said as he stepped into the flat, smiling at her then looking around, "nice place." He handed a bag of pastries that smelled divine to Nick and held out his hand.

"Ares," she took it, and his fingers tightened around hers, though whether he was trying to warn her, or size her up, or had noticed that she was somehow different from the day before she couldn't tell.

"All right, I'm out of here," he said, dropping her hand.

"You aren't staying?" she asked.

"And get in the way of you two love-birds? I don't think so.

"Besides, I've errands to run.

"Catch ya later!"

He turned and Nick transferred the bakery bag to his left hand and with his right, did a complicated handshake with Ares involving fist bumps, standard handshakes, thumb handshakes and shoulder taps.

And then she was alone with Nick.

At least she was fully dressed this time, but not sure whether to fold her hands in front of her groin, or fold her arms, or swing her arms or turn away.

"He's right," Nick said.

"About what?"

"It is a nice place, but not one where the beige version of you would be comfortable."

He went back into her little kitchen, put the pastries on a plate from the dish rack and started opening cupboards looking for another coffee cup, only there wasn't one.

"You have the cup, I'll take the glass," she went to the table to fetch it.

"You only have one cup?"

"I'm not here much."

"Why not?" he asked, pouring the coffee.

She gestured around the room, "I work a lot, and this place is too small to have many people around, so I just meet up elsewhere."

"Your cocoon," he looked around the flat again, this time noting the singles; one small couch, with one cushion and throw rug, one table.

One screen, partly obscuring a bed that hadn't been made yet.

And yet, it was comfortable, with art on the walls, and collections of shells, ceramics and tiny animal sculptures. And dammit he was right; it was her cocoon.

"Doesn't take much to clean," she said brightly.

He turned back to her.

She carried the plate to the table, and he carried the drinks.

They looked at each other and subsided into the couch.

Which only had one bum print in its centre, and as he settled on the left, and her on the right, the stuffing shifted throwing them closer together.

He cleared his throat and adjusted his seating a little further away.

"Are these yours?" he asked, gesturing at a couple of large landscapes she'd been trying to figure out how to use as room dividers.

She nodded.

"You're very talented." He looked around again, "may I look at your other sketchbooks?"

"No."

"Modest?"

"Not really, you can see there isn't much room here so I have a storage unit," she lied.

Wilkinson's bought the sketchbooks, new ones for each investigation so of course, she gave them back when they filled up.

He offered her the plate; she picked up a pastry and took a bite.

"You're the first person I've given a book to, but now I've got the idea I might be able to sell them," which was *technically* correct.

He chose a pastry and took a bite.

It occurred to her that she wasn't supposed to know anything about him, except that he was pretty enough to follow around for days trying to get a good picture.

And that she was getting a pay rise to find out more about him.

Which left her feeling uncomfortable, and a little dirty.

Even if he was a crime kingpin.

Clearly, she was not cut out for law enforcement.

"So, you know I go around drawing total strangers, what is it you do for a living?"

He laughed, "nothing as exciting as sketching strangers. I sell professional espresso coffee machines and supplies."

"Is it a good living?"

"Of course! This is Melbourne, home of the world's best coffee culture after all.

"Getting the distribution agreements with the overseas manufacturers was the hardest part, but pretty much everyone in business here is looking to buy or lease them.

"It's not just cafés and restaurants, I've got high-end boutiques, barbers and car repair services signed up too. I even had a plastic surgeon sign up for one yesterday!"

"A plastic surgeon? That's a road too far for me, but sometimes it can take hours at the hairdresser and I reckon a decent coffee would help the wait."

He ran a sticky finger along a lock of her hair, "you spend hours in a hairdresser to get this look?"

"It was for a wedding, okay?"

He stuffed the pasty in his mouth and held his hands out looking for something to wipe them with.

She swallowed the rest of her coffee, leaving the glass in the kitchen, brought him back the dish towel.

When she thought about it, every place she'd sketched him, sold coffee. It was a *very* good cover story.

The doorbell went, so she left him on the couch while she answered it.

"Package for delivery," Ryan said, "please sign here."

She stepped through to the corridor, and he quietly said, "it's a combined bug and panic button; I've activated it for you. If you can speak, say "Quetzal-coatl," and we'll know you're in trouble. Just press the head of the serpent to activate the alarm, and we'll come get you."

She nodded.

"Don't worry, we'll be nearby."

She smiled a thin, straight smile.

"Thanks very much," she called out as he left, and started unwrapping the parcel as she returned to the flat.

She shoved the wrapping in the pocket of her jeans, pinned the brooch to her right shoulder, and twisted her body back and forth, enjoying its sparkle in the changing light.

"That's pretty," Nick said, coming up behind her.

"I saw it online and paid full price before it could get away."

"Is that Quetzalcoatl?"

She didn't start, or pause, just said, "sure is," as she took his hand and walked back to the couch, settling in on his left where, hopefully, the bug would pick him up well.

"Tell me more about your coffee business."

Nick smiled, as though it was a topic he couldn't get enough of.

"Well, if I was selling you one, I'd want to know how many cups you'd be making, what kinds of coffee, and how much effort to put into them."

"And want if I didn't want to make any effort at all?"

"Then I'd get you the fully automatic push-button kind and have it plumbed into the main water pipe. Then you'd just have to fill up the milk powder and sugar when it ran out."

"What if I wanted to make "proper" lattes for people?"

"If you were making coffees all day, then I'd suggest a machine with a heat exchanger, or if you were really concerned about an exact temperature of coffee a multi-boiler.

"You need something like 25 amps of power for the heat exchanger and up to 40 for a boiler.

"And a two-group head for about 20 kg of coffee a week, or three groups for up to 100 kg a week.

"You've got machines where you can program shots by weight, and others that auto-brew.

"Plus, I'd recommend an automatic cleaning cycle and an overnight mode that powers down when you haven't used it for a while.

"And let's not forget the ergonomic stress of using it all, so you want to think about bench height, and comfortable handles, and anti-fatigue mats."

"Or coffee for twelve in one go?"

"Drip filter style. The beauty of this kind is that you don't need to plug it in the main water, just add fresh water."

It sounded plausible, but he hadn't said anything she couldn't have figured out by herself with an internet search.

And she didn't have enough knowledge to ask him the right questions to trap him.

"What about Ares?"

"I saved his life, and when he fell on hard times, I hired him; he drives me around, helps me move the stock, and does other bits and pieces."

She nodded, plausible.

"What about you? What kind of job do you have that gives you the time to follow me around for days?"

"Actually, I've fallen on hard times myself - I'm between jobs. Taking a week off before looking for something else."

She hated lying, but how else was she supposed to explain it? It wasn't the kind of thing "normal" people did.

They sat silently for a moment. Nick looked around again, and Susan was relieved she hadn't room for anything much more than small, second-hand furniture. There wasn't anything there to suggest a good job, just junk.

If he asked what kind of job, what should she say?

Or would he be worried she was going to ask him for a job?

He cleared his throat again. "So, who was on the phone then?"

"When?"

"Just then, you said 'I don't have a choice, he's right here at my door.'"

And reminded her of the stakes again.

Nick Liang was supposed to be the kind of guy who would beat you up as soon as look at you.

She had to remember that, no matter how nice and, well, innocent he seemed.

"Oh that," she manufactured a giggle, "I was just telling my friend about you. She was warning me to steer clear."

They smiled at each other for a moment.

Susan, forgetting for a moment she was drinking from a glass she'd left in the kitchen, lunged for his coffee before he could do something worrying, like kiss her.

His phone rang, breaking the tension and bring some breathing space.

He glanced at it, and said, "sorry, I have to get this," before getting off the couch and walking out the door.

She snuck after him, trying to eavesdrop on the conversation.

"Yes," he said, followed by grunting interspersed by periods when someone at the other end said something.

Difficult to read much into that, until he said, "I'll be there as soon as I can."

Fortunately, she had enough time to get into the kitchen and look like she was busy.

"I'm sorry," he said, "I've got to go. There's a thing..."

"Oh. Well. Okay then. I'll see you sometime."

"Can, um, can I call you?"

"What, oh yeah, I guess."

And then, blessedly, he was gone.

Presumably taking Ryan and whoever had replaced her on surveillance detail.

Leaving a space behind that was ridiculously big for someone who'd barely been there an hour.

But having been that close to him, she didn't think he the same air of lethality Aresio did.

The original team briefing hadn't detailed much of the kind of information you'd think a person who'd killed another person with his bare hands would accrue.

It was as if he'd suddenly appeared, with no gang affiliation or history to explain who he was and where he'd come from.

He'd emerged fully formed out of nowhere. Without a supervillain origin story if you will.

She decided to do some digging on her own, and pulled her laptop out from its storage place under the couch, logging into her account at Wilkinson's and searching all the databases available to her; publicly and through Wilkinson's subscriptions.

Sometime later, she'd come with back plenty over the last five years or so, and next to nothing previously.

Not high school records, not immigration records, not even a library card.

It would have done for the most cursory background check, but not for someone like her, or someone using the specialised skills at Wilkinson's.

For comparison, she searched Aresio, found a number of aliases, criminal activity dating back more than a decade, as well as school records.

She rang Mimma, who asked, "how are you getting on with the target? Any issues I need to know about?"

"Fine, he's left me to do something, but I expect Ryan is tailing him.

"But something's not right, and I'm not sure I can explain it."

"What makes you say that?"

Susan settled herself more comfortably on the couch, "what exactly do we know about our client, and what exactly do we know about Nick Liang?"

"We haven't backgrounded the client, and our basic starting point is always that the client is honest with us. The fee for engagement generally ensures only serious queries."

"Has anyone authorised a full background search on Nick Liang to confirm the details we've been given?"

"I couldn't say for sure, that wasn't part of my briefing. Why?"

"I've done some basic background, and his history is quite short. On the other hand, his friend Aresio Vitale has a long history."

"What are you saying?" Mimma was starting to sound annoyed.

"I'm wondering whether Nick Liang exists, or whether he's an undercover operative sent by the AFP, or ASIO.

"Perhaps to investigate Aresio?"

Mimma was silent, Susan could almost hear Mimma's brain moving.

Susan continued, "the client may be suspicious of Nick's credentials, and if he's undercover, we may be putting his life in danger."

Susan waited another moment or two before Mimma sighed.

"Let me check with Ben. I'll get back to you."

It was several days before she heard from Mimma, but in the meantime, she'd watched the news break as the AFP busted an international drug ring in conjunction with Police in 16 other countries.

They'd seized more than 105 kg of drugs, 42 firearms, more than 9.5 million dollars in cash, plus luxury goods and cars in Victoria alone. As well as evidence of 19 murder plots in ongoing investigations.

Prominent footage included Aresio wearing handcuffs, escorted by Police, plus others with covers over their heads.

No sign or mention of Nick though.

And when she got her next pay, it included exactly 2.8 days of higher duties, most of which was gobbled up in the extra tax.

According to Mimma, Ben had contacted someone he knew in the intelligence community, and shared some information about the investigation. And that was about all she permitted to know.

Presumably, they'd gotten him out.

Life continued pretty much as normal. She took her sketchbooks from Wilkinson's and dressed in her beige sundress as she continued to sketch her assigned targets.

As the weather cooled, she added a beige cardigan and sought warmer observation points than benches in the Bourke Street Mall.

She tried harder to blend into the crowds, but her heart wasn't really in it.

And she kept seeing Nick everywhere. Though she was fairly sure that was her imagination.

He'd given her a glimpse of an alternative future. Not so much the gangster's moll element, more the like-minded... Soul mate?

Gak.

She definitely needed a holiday somewhere sunny and frenzied, followed by a transfer to another department.

Someone took a seat next to her, but as the café was filling up for the lunch crowd, she just shifted her chair enough to clear her view of the target.

"Did you forget me so soon?" a voice asked?

She looked up to see Nick. Only also not Nick.

He'd cut his hair, and dressed in jeans and a button-down shirt with the sleeves rolled up, looked less like a gangster and more like the Police officer she'd supposed him to be.

"You still owe me a drink," he said.

She didn't know what to say, so she didn't say anything.

He stood up and offered her his hand.

She looked past him to Ryan on the other side of the café, and made a seemingly random coded gesture to let him know she was off.

Then looked back up at Nick, and said "fine.

"You owe me an explanation."

"If I didn't owe you my life, I'd be demanding an explanation."

She smiled, and took his hand, "let's get a drink and you can tell me all about it."

THE END

THE LAST CASE

It was the kind of beautiful, crisp, clear winter's day that Lily White loved. She walked down the grass verge beside the path, enjoying the crunching of frost beneath her boots, and as she turned the corner, the sight of a single set of footprints descending the hill.

She loved snuggling into her hat and scarf, the cold biting at the tops of her cheeks as she started walking.

And she loved unravelling the scarf and opening her bright blue overcoat as she got to the bottom of the hill and warmed up.

Then wrapping herself up again as she waited at the train station, and unravelling as the carriage filled up with passengers and the temperature rose.

But most of all, she loved watching the hot air balloons, suspended in the cloudless sky above Melbourne as her train approached the city.

As was her custom, she ordered a latte at the café downstairs, checked the mailbox, and bounded up the three flights of stairs rather than waiting for the ancient lift.

The Nicholas Building was completed in 1926; the stairs wound tightly around the lift well and were the perfect height for comfortably climbing. Even for someone as petite as Lily.

As she reached her floor, she paused to admire the varnished red wood solidity of her door, as she pulled the key from her pocket and turned it in the old, worn, brass deadlock.

"I'm here Gramps," she called as she opened the door.

He didn't answer, but that wasn't really a surprise. He'd been out on a surveillance job the night before and might have stopped off to freshen up and take a nap on the way in.

She put the mail on her desk, noticed the answering machine wasn't flashing messages waiting to be heard, then took a sip of coffee and turned the ancient heater on.

Lily was just warm enough from the run up the stairs to take her outer layers off, knowing the heater would have warmed up by the point she was about ready to put them back on again.

The down side of an older building was the old black steel crittal window frames. They looked beautiful but had absolutely no thermal properties.

Not to worry, Gramps said she was a softy just like all young people today. He himself was of an age where he thought fresh air was more important than heat and always kept the windows a tiny bit open.

And they did look lovely set against the white walls, so perhaps in this instance, form trumped function.

The office was decorated with what passed for Sherlock Holmes-style furniture in the 1940s.

As you walked in the door, to your right was her desk, a non-adjustable real wood desk with one big drawer under the main writing surface, and smaller drawers down the right-hand side that meant she had to use a footstool and a cushion on the chair to reach a comfortable height.

She'd always meant to get a proper ergonomic chair, but as tiny as she was, she'd almost certainly need a custom make. The idea of a child-size office desk and chair was more than she could cope with.

Next to the desk, between the wall and the desk, was a low, lateral filing cabinet that held their archived cases. She used its top for her trays and the phone.

On the other side, the waiting room consisted of a slim, wood-framed burgundy upholstered lounge suite of coffee table, two armchairs and a sofa.

When Gran insisted on upgrading their household furniture, it had been sent to the office.

Gramps sometimes napped on the couch though he was too tall to rest up comfortably.

The magazines were only a decade or so out of date.

On a normal day, she liked to dress a little bit retro, in keeping with the era. Nothing obvious, just heels, a pencil skirt and blouse.

The room smelled of Gramps' cigars, and very faintly of the beeswax and lavender furniture polish Gran used to use.

Even when building management forbade smoking in the building, he opened the windows and leant on the wall, looking down on the street to enjoy his cigar and whisky at the end of the day.

Overall, the office looked like a film set, with the morning sun shining through the wood and mottled glass wall dividing the front from Gramps at the back. Highlighting the letters painstakingly painted onto the door with a golden glow that was only half in her imagination.

Lewis White
Private Investigator

According to Gran, it was his colleagues at the Wilkinson National Detective Agency who'd paid to have the sign on the door when he'd left.

She took another sip of coffee, and pulled her laptop out of the filing cabinet, opening it and turning it on before taking the day's newspaper back to put on his desk.

She opened the partition door and was shocked into stillness at the condition of the room.

It was an utter shambles; furniture overturned, papers fanned out across the floor, and even odder, Gramps' jacket and hat, still on the overturned hat rack.

There was no way he'd left the office in that condition.

She shut the door, retreated to her desk, and called the Police.

Not too much later, a young constable arrived to take stock of the scene. He was cute if you liked big blond-haired, blue-eyed guys.

Which Lily did.

"Constable Declan Gill," he introduced himself.

"Private Investigator Lily White," she said offering her hand.

Constable Gill took out his notebook, "what seems to be the trouble here."

Lily opened the door, and indicated the mess inside, "we've been burgled; this room was as neat as the other when I left last night."

The constable looked from the messy room to the tidy room. "What was taken?"

"I haven't had a chance to look. I thought you'd need to get the crime scene guys in before I checked or something."

A smile chased across his face and was gone almost before she noticed, "do you have any cameras here in the office, or on this floor?"

"Aaahh. No. I think there might be some in the elevators and on the ground floor to protect the stained-glass ceilings, but not up here."

"I see, and did you see anyone when you left last night?"

"The tenants on this side were gone, but I think there might have been someone on the other side, I could see a light. I didn't see any people waiting around though."

He stood in the doorway, looking around the room, "no footprints, no obvious contaminants." He pulled a little fingerprint kit from a pocket in his utility vest and stepped through the door to dust a few test surfaces including the sides of the bookshelves and desk.

"Whoever did this was likely wearing gloves," he turned to look at her, "I'll take the report back, but I have to be honest with you. If you can't tell me exactly what was taken, and even if you do, it's unlikely anything further will come of this report."

If Lily was honest, she was annoyed with how offhand the constable was.

And once he'd gone, and she looked through the door at the mess again, she realised he had a point.

She had no idea whether anything was missing.

And no idea where to start looking for it. Starting seemed more problematic than finishing.

Perhaps if she started putting things back in order, she'd be better able to tell what was missing.

But she'd need some more appropriate clothes for moving the furniture, and luckily, she'd forgotten to take her gym clothes home. Several times...

After a quick trip to the lady's toilet downstairs, she was ready to wade into the mess of Gramps' office.

First, she closed the laptop and stacked it with the mail and phone on top of the trays, which she stacked one on top of the other. She picked up the hat rack and carried it behind her desk next to the filing cabinet, smoothing Gramps' jacket down and carefully placing his hat on the top.

Then she started picking up the books, papers and ornaments, randomly stacking them on and around her desk and the filing cabinet. Followed by the chairs and coffee table as well.

When the floor was mostly clear, it was time to start righting the furniture.

At which point, it became clear what the limitations of her 148 cm frame were.

She saw Gramps' half-full whisky bottle in the corner. Perhaps a tot of whisky might give her the strength she needed.

She'd just taken a swig from the bottle, and was appreciating the burn in her throat, (which overlaid the desire to cry tears of frustration) when someone cleared their throat behind her.

As she swung around, she hid the bottle and lid behind her back.

It was the young constable again, taking in the changes the last couple of hours had made.

Kind enough to ignore the whisky, though he must have seen it.

"Er, you might need another of those Miss White."

She brazened it out, putting the stopper on the whisky and easing it onto the corner of her desk, "you couldn't give me a hand with this," she stuck her thumb over her right shoulder to indicate the office, "could you?"

"Urm, we're really not supposed to...

"Sure, why not."

He walked into the room and took hold of a bookshelf, "just back against the wall?"

"Yes," she said, following him in.

He heaved the shelf up.

"Careful," she said, as books that had previously been held in by the leg of the desk cascaded down.

She hesitated for a moment before sweeping them out of the way with a foot and moving to help with the next bookshelf and then the last.

Drawers had spilled out of the desk, so they stacked them in a corner before setting that right.

Then emptying Gramps' old filing cabinets because it was easier to lift them that way.

"Does anything look to be missing?" he asked.

Lily sighed and wiped a smear of dust across her forehead, "Now you ask?" she looked around, "I can't really tell without putting it all back."

"Come sit down," he said, pulling her into the waiting room and moving a stack of papers from one of the armchairs to the floor nearby, "there's something I need to tell you."

And moving a stack from the other so he could drag it closer to her.

She got up to pull a bottle of water from her bag and take a drink.

Constable Gill took a deep breath, "I have some bad news for you," he looked into her face, gauging her reaction.

"This morning we were called to a scene in Essendon where we found Mr Lewis, deceased, in his car. The coroner believes the cause of death may have been a heart attack."

The colour drained from Lily's face, and Declan caught the water bottle as she lifted her hands to her face.

"The death is not considered suspicious at this stage," he said screwing the lid back on, "but I have to ask you whether you know what he was doing in Essendon."

Lily scrubbed her face with her hands, and took a deep breath, "I'll need to check the computer."

She climbed to her feet, and almost slid over a stack of papers. He leapt to his feet and pushed her back into the chair, "I'll go."

He brought her laptop over, opening the lid for her.

She crossed her legs on the armchair and typed her password to gain entry to the system, but there was nothing there.

No programmes.

No files.

Absolutely nothing there.

She checked the recycle bin on the landing page, and that was empty too.

She slapped the keys with both hands in frustration, and still nothing.

She turned it over, looking at the case. It appeared to be her laptop, with the ancient cute puppy sticker still affixed, though that didn't mean that the innards hadn't been replaced.

"It's empty," she said stupidly.

"May I look?" he asked.

She handed it over, "why would someone do that? I can't imagine anyone on the kind of domestic scale we specialise in making that much effort."

"Oh, people can get—"

"Wouldn't they rather throw the goddammed thing on the floor and hit it with a baseball bat a couple of times.?"

"It seems more deliberate than that—"

"But his office was just trashed... Maybe they were angry when they couldn't find whatever it was on the one and only computer in the office."

"Then it's gone forever, and we won't know for sure why."

Lily cackled like a witch, and Declan looked at her sharply.

"No it isn't, I have a backup. I take a backup every day; one in the cloud and one on an external drive I take away with me."

"You do what?"

"Yes," she grinned, "there was an incident with faulty wiring a few years ago and we lost everything. I wasn't taking that chance again. It took forever to recreate the files."

"Then I'll just take the drive back to the office."

And that was it, back on the case - Lily would let herself grieve later.

"No you won't. Not without a warrant. I need the details on the backup to reconstruct the cases."

"Surely you can let it go and let the Police take over now."

"No, I can't. I have responsibilities to our clients; they've paid good money to resolve the issues that matter to them."

"Aren't you just the receptionist?"

She laughed, a genuine laugh, as though he'd told a great joke.

"Is that what you think? That's too precious." She snapped the laptop shut and walked to the desk, clearing a space to lay it down, hardly bothered that half the papers she'd laboriously stacked it with earlier fell on the floor.

"But I thought..."

"We're actually the White Family Investigations." She rifled through her handbag until she found her wallet, and pulled a card from it, "I told you before, Private Investigator," and flicked him her license.

"I do the online stuff," she said, connecting her external drive, "and Gramps does the real world."

He didn't correct her on the tense.

"Before he died," she started typing, "Dad did the computer stuff until I came on board. Mum and Gran were the receptionists in the old days, but they're both gone now too."

He handed her back the card, "so what's next?"

She paused, waiting for the laptop to access the drive's data, "well, I'll close out the old cases, and probably move the business closer to home. Or at least I will when I get my Private Security Business Licence," she said smiling at him.

She started typing again.

"Now, let's see. He was working on a couple of things...

"Lost dog in Heidelberg, art theft in Moonee Ponds, missing person in Northcote, so nothing that close to Essendon."

She ran her hands through her hair, "this would be so much easier if I had his daybook. It's where he notes all the information about his day - who he's spoken to, what cases he takes, and so on. I'd be able to check where he was up to on his current cases, and why he was in Essendon last night."

She paused to look at him, "unless he just stopped for a bit of shopping?"

He shook his head slightly, "even if it's in his car, it will be held as evidence until we can confirm the cause of death."

She frowned at him, "even if you do, you won't be able to read it. It's in code, and I'd appreciate it back as soon as possible."

She typed for a moment more, then stopped to look at him, "is there anything else you need?"

"What? Oh. No. There's nothing else Police-wise, though you may need to come down to the station to make a statement. The office, and laptop drive, in conjunction with the deceased, make a suspicious series of events."

"Well," she said, "don't let me keep you from your investigations, I can manage the rest on my own."

"Are you sure?"

"Of course, you've done the hard stuff."

He took a step back from the desk, "all right. But you'll let me know when you find out if anything's missing?"

"Of course."

He walked to the door, and paused before passing through it, "may I call in tomorrow to see how you're getting on?"

She smiled, "of course. I'd like that."

She watched him leave, and waited a minute or two more, before allowing herself a moment or two to stand by the window, allowing her eyes to blur over.

Gramps was dead, and she was all alone in the world.

And then she pulled herself together. Pulling her track pants up and redoing the ties before pulling her t-shirt down.

She had three cases to look into, not to mention getting to the bottom of Gramps' death.

Then she could let herself fall into grief.

But first, lunch.

Somewhere else.

She locked the office, walked down the stairs, and out into the street, trotting down a nearby alleyway until she came to a small food court where she ordered a big bowl of noodles and a small glass of wine.

Pulling out her daybook, she tried to make sense of the day.

Hard drive wiped

Office trashed

G dead at Essendon

Cases Heidelberg, Moonee Ponds, Northcote

Dog, painting, missing person

What she hadn't mentioned to Declan, was that the missing person was a personal case.

Someone Gramps had lost contact with when he'd fallen in with a bad crowd.

Someone Gramps had been fairly sure had been murdered.

Not that it mattered, she hadn't been lying when she said she needed his daybook to see where he was up to.

In the meantime, there was still the matter of finding out if anything else had been stolen from the office. She finished up her lunch and left.

When she got back to the office, she started by checking all the surfaces of the desk and book-shelves; inspired by old detective shows where the thing you were looking for was taped underneath the desk, but not finding anything.

So much for that then.

When she got all the books back on the shelves, she discovered some of them were missing. And with all the ornaments and souvenirs back in place, there were a few pieces not accounted for when she'd pieced together enough of the fragments to see what was there.

She'd almost cried over the remains of the "World's Best Detective" mug that came from his Wilkinson's colleagues as well.

But with the office more or less in order once again, it looked weirdly empty without Gramps in it.

There were still the stacks of paper to go through, but by that point, she was exhausted.

Reorganising the office had been the last thing on her mind when she arrived that morning.

She didn't even bother to get changed, just threw on her overcoat and went home.

She spent more of the night awake than asleep, and in the end, got up early and caught the train back into town.

Dressed more practically in jeans, sneakers and a thick fleece jacket.

She was on the way so early, the train never really filled up, and there was next to no one about.

Even her café hadn't opened its doors - they told her to come back in half an hour when the espresso machine had warmed up.

She stood in the doorway, trying to see and feel whether anything was different. Or what it was that had prevented her from settling.

There was just the usual, with papers stacked all over the desk and chairs and the floor.

And then it hit her - she hadn't checked her desk.

Someone had to have got into her filing cabinet to get at the laptop. And maybe they'd started with the desk.

She smoothed a hand down the sides of her drawers to discover someone had jimmied the lock, which was a bit funny because she'd never locked it. The wood had warped and it was all about the technique of pulling them out.

She pulled all the drawers out and felt around in the cavities.

Something had been taped to the underside of the desk, so she pulled it out, unwrapped it to find a thumb drive.

She left it aside for the moment, and checked all the sides of the drawers, taking a quick look to see that nothing appeared to be missing, (and discovering a few items she thought had been lost).

She took her laptop out of the filing cabinet and plugged the thumb drive into it, giving it a moment to connect while she flicked through the folders to see if anything was missing.

It looked fine, but she wasn't actually confident she could remember everything that was in there.

She'd been planning to send a bunch of stuff to their archival storage but hadn't quite got a box full.

And wasn't real keen on paying to send and store one that wasn't.

The laptop made the kind of whirl that indicated it had connected to the drive, so she opened it up to find a load of photographs, dated a couple of weeks ago.

She opened one at random, and it showed two men fighting in some kind of alleyway at night. She opened another to see the two again, only the lighting and focus was slightly better, and the man on the left was looking a bit worse for wear.

And another where the only reason he was upright, was because the other man was holding his shirt, his arm drawn back to punch him.

In the next, he was slumped on the ground, and the other walking away, turning his head backwards to spit.

She wasn't entirely sure what she was seeing, so she went back to the first in the series and flicked through them one at a time to show what was beginning to look like a murder.

She looked around the office, suddenly feeling cold, and realising she hadn't turned the heater on.

But still feeling she was being watched.

She pulled the drive from the laptop and slipped it into her jacket pocket.

She was just locking the door again when she heard the lift clanking as it approached the floor and came to a stop.

She raced down the corridor and around the corner so whoever was coming up didn't see her.

And when she heard to door to the lift well close, back around to the other side to run down the stairs.

In case there was a lookout, she went through the café, and ducked out the street entrance.

She ran the two city blocks to the East Melbourne police station, not daring to look back for signs of pursuit; hoping it was Declan's station, and he would be there.

She bent over just inside the door gasping for air, trying to see down the street.

"Can I help you Ma'am?"

She turned to see a female officer at the reception counter, "Ma'am?"

"Declan," she gasped, trying to get her breathing back under control, "Constable Declan Gill."

"One moment," she said, walking through a door separating the back office from the front reception counter.

After a few seconds, she was more or less under control and took a seat to wait. Swinging her legs a little as she waited.

And after a short eternity, he came to meet her.

Wordlessly she held out the drive to him.

He nodded, "would you come with me please?"

He put her in a small room, "coffee?"

She nodded, and he left her for a few moments before returning with a small, milky, sugary vending machine cup.

She looked at him doubtfully.

"It's not the best, but it's what we have," he said, "wait here and I'll see the detective."

Another short eternity and he arrived with a detective carrying a laptop and a file.

"Detective Fiona Harrison," she said, "do you mind if I ask you a few questions?"

She glanced at Declan, who nodded slightly, then said, "of course."

The detective gestured to the door, and escorted her to an interview room.

"You are..." she looked in her file, "Lily White of White Family Investigations?"

"Yes."

"You are the Granddaughter of Lewis White deceased?"

"Yes."

"You reported a break-in at your offices in the Nicholas Building?"

"Yes."

"And at that time, all that you could say for sure was missing, was the contents of your laptop?"

"Yes."

"You arrived this morning with this thumb drive?" she held up what looked like the thumb drive in a small, sealed plastic bag with a couple of signatures across the seal.

"I can't be sure it's the *same* drive, but it looks like the one I discovered taped underneath my desk this morning, and ran down the street to the station with."

The detective rolled her eyes, then opened up the laptop to reveal one of the photos in the series, "do these photos look familiar?"

"Yes, it looks like one of the ones I discovered on the thumb drive."

"And can you identify either the two main combatants or any of the others in the photograph?"

Lily had only noticed the characters in the foreground, so she leaned forward to look at the men watching along the side-lines.

"Ummm, no, I don't think so."

"What about the location?"

Lily looked again, thinking it might have been the alleyway behind the building, but she didn't recognise it.

"No."

"And do you know what they're doing in this picture?"

She glanced at Declan again before she answered, "illegal street fight? Gang justice? Football rivalry?"

"Can you think of any reason why Mr White might have had this in his possession?"

"Evidence obviously."

"Of what?"

"How would I know? I only know of three ongoing investigations; lost dog in Heidelberg, art theft in Moonee Ponds, and a missing person in Northcote.

"These photos might have been taken for any one of them. Or simply be something he saw while he was out somewhere else.

"If I had his daybook, I could check whether he wrote anything down about them."

The detective opened the file and pulled out a notebook, encased in an evidence bag. "Is this the daybook you're referring to?"

"Yes."

The detective broke the seal and handed it to Lily, who flicked through the pages until she got to the one with the date of the photographs.

"Let's see..."

"What language is that?" asked the detective.

"What? Oh," Lily laughed and marked her place on the page with a finger, "it's Elvish. Gramps was really taken with *The Lord of the Rings*, and taught himself the runes. Next to no one can read any further than the return address if they find one of the daybooks. We all had to learn.

"Ah, while I think of it, was his camera kit in the car when you found it? There might be more recent evidence in there."

The room went still, "I see. You didn't find the camera."

She went back to the book and kept reading, flipping through a few pages before and after.

"No, nothing about the photos, though he did find the missing artwork and return it, so now I can close that one off and send them their final invoice."

"What about the last few days. Was there anything that made him think hiding the drive was a good idea?"

Lily kept reading, "no mention of it. I wonder if he thought to keep me safe by not writing it down.

"Or was he attempting to blackmail that guy? I can't think why he would do that.

"Maybe he was holding it for someone..."

She flipped back a few pages and started reading again, "could this have been the "artwork" he retrieved?"

She glanced up at the detective, who had a weird look on her face, half incredulity, half pity, "what?"

"Do you know who Leo Palleschi is?"

"No. Should I?"

She tapped the big man in the photo, "this is Leo Palleschi, he's a relatively well-known gang enforcer."

"Ah. I'm beginning to get the picture."

"Did Gramps really die of a heart attack?"

"Yes, it's been confirmed. There are some postmortem injuries, so perhaps he saw Palleschi coming and died of fright."

"I see."

Lily gulped down the remains of her cold, unpalatable coffee.

"Am I in danger?"

"That rather depends on who wanted the pictures.

"Any chance you could take a vacation?"

"Are you planning to use my office as a trap?"

"We might."

"Do I have any choice?"

"Of course you do, but I imagine you'd like to catch whoever's responsible for your grandfather's death. And to be able to resume your work without fear of reprisals?"

There was no *real* choice.

"Constable Gill can escort you back to the premises to collect your things, then take you home."

《《　•　》》

It was a little over a week before she was permitted to re-enter the office.

She stood outside the door, wiping her hands down her jeans, afraid of what she might see when she opened the door.

She took a deep breath, closed her eyes, and flung the door open.

It appeared more or less as it had before all this happened. Neat and clean, though she had no idea where all the papers went.

A large bunch of flowers almost engulfed the coffee table, and on the desk was a large stack of mail.

She couldn't face opening the inner door just yet. She knew when she did, she'd see Gramps turning to meet her with his wild white hair and three-piece suit. So she left it shut, and moved to her desk, dumping her bag and the mail on the filing cabinet.

Lily sighed and wondered who would drop Gramps things back, and when.

And then she sighed and thought about all the work closing the office down entailed.

And then there was a tentative knock on the door, so faint she barely heard it.

Lily got up to open it and startled a woman a couple of paces back.

"Can I help you?"

"Is this White Family Investigations?"

"Yes it is, would you like to come in?"

"Oh, I'm not sure... I only... I..."

"Come and sit down, tell me what it is you're worried about?"

"Well, I..."

"At least come in away from prying eyes."

The woman sat on the edge of an armchair; her handbag cradled in her lap. "Well, you see. My boyfriend borrowed some money, and now he's stopped answering his phone, and I'm worried something terrible has happened to him."

The Last Case

And just like that, she was on a new case. There would be plenty of time to take care of the office.

THE END

Alexandria Blaelock writes stories, some of them for *Ellery Queen's Mystery Magazine* and *Pulphouse Fiction Magazine*.

She's also written five self-help books applying business techniques to personal matters like getting dressed, cleaning house, and feeding your friends.

She lives in a forest because she enjoys birdsong, the scent of gum leaves and the sun on her face. When not telecommuting to parallel universes from her Melbourne based imagination, she watches K-dramas, talks to animals, and drinks Campari. At the same time.

Discover more at www.alexandriablaelock.com